INCARCERATION OF TEARS

A Collection of Poems, Personal Essays and Short Story

TERREL CARTER

iDream Publications
INCARCERATION OF TEAR
Available for purchase from Amazon.com and other retail outlets
© 2014 by Terrel Carter

"Incarceration of Tears" first appeared on the blog Minutes before Six, February 13, 2014. "Lord What Was I Thinking" first appeared in Guilty Reflections (revised edition) 2012. "To Catch a Shadow" first appeared on the blog Minutes before Six, September 13, 2013.

ISBN-13:978-0983596530
ISBN-10:0983596530
Cover Design: Strickly Graphics
Text Formation: Stacey Woolfolk
Copy Editing:Eduard Ramirez, Vernon Robinson, and Tonya Skief
Interior Photos: Ashley Bald
Published by: iDream Publications
P.O. Box 24197
Philadelphia, PA 19139

PRINTED IN THE UNITED STATES OF AMERICA

DEDICATION

To My Daughter Shante,

For most of your life I haven't been around to be the father that you needed me to be. I've apologized a thousand times, but apologies are just words, they can't take away the pain of being without your father. So, I've dedicated this book to you—a small token of my unconditional love. This is my gift, along with the hope that I'll be with you soon, to make up for all the time I've missed.

ACKNOWLEDGEMENTS

For those of us confined, no matter what that confinement might be, writing is an expression of freedom. It allows us to stretch our wings of creative expression so that we may soar beyond the walls that confine us.

To everyone who helped with this book, I offer my profound gratitude: My wife, Stacey, who pushed through her frustrations to make it happen. My mother, Tonya and my sisters Kim and Kalima who without their encouragement and support I would be lost. To my brothers, Muhammed and Masai hold your heads up and stretch out those wings of imagination. To my friends: Eddie Ramirez who helped bring out the best in me, Giovanni Reid who's been my sounding board, Jamo, Lil Charlie, Vern, Walt, Rasul, Sadique, Faheem, Boo, Lou Banks, Ghani and Muti, the struggle is our life and we will succeed. And last but not least, Lori and Trish, thanks for your insight.

TABLE OF CONTENTS

LORD, WHAT WAS I THINKING?

Lord, what was I thinking?
Or was I even thinking at all?
A manchild suffering from a malady
caught vulnerable and unaware
by the pulse of a city strip.
The city throbbed with a steady rhythm
a vibration invasion
that penetrated deep.
Like a moth
I was drawn to the synthetic glow
that corrupted the nighttime skies,
my young eyes were blinded
by the glitter of jewels
that rested upon dark flesh,
like stars sparkling against
the backdrop of space.
Walking billboards of fashion designers
advertising self-esteem was just
the medication I needed
to cure this malaise of self-hatred
"Am I good now"?
Or am I feeling
the ill effects of the "feel good"
the alcohol, the pills, the codeine,
the weed…

Lord, what was I thinking?
Or was I even thinking at all?
I followed false trails to manhood
defined by boys without
a clue as to where those trails would lead,
all along the way
kicking cocaine vials
like broken-off pieces of cement...
A young man who flew too close to the sun
setting his wings on fire.

Lord, what was I thinking?
Or was I even thinking at all?
Sprouting up through the cracks of concrete
flowers of womanhood
blossomed like it was
springtime in a meadow.
I picked, I pulled, I uprooted.
Only to own, only to possess.
Not to love, not to admire,
not to protect.
But to lose myself in pleasures
that lasted only a moment
then passed as quickly as a dream
leaving behind a trail
of broken hearts and shattered self-esteems.

Lord, what was I thinking?
Or was I even thinking at all?
Defined and marginalized,
boxed in and boxed out.

I was the hardest person
in the world to know
a stranger to myself.
Only to discover who I am
at the cost of everything
I held dear.
Now my nights are haunted
by echoes of my ancestors
crying out in shame,
"Oh son, what have you done?"
Couldn't you hear
the rattling of the chains?"

Oh Lord, what was I thinking?
Or was I even thinking at all?

I was six years old when the bulldozers came. The rumble of their engines and their huge tires rolling over the uneven ground of the empty lot behind my home awakened me from my sleep. Startled, I jumped from my bed and raced to my window. Mechanical monsters cut wide swaths through the weeds, their exhaust pipes blew smoke like the flaring nostrils of a hungry dragon and their shovels, like the mouth of some pre-historic beast filled with dagger-like teeth, bit out huge chunks of earth as if it were the flesh of its prey. Tears flowed from my eyes because this wasn't just any old empty lot. This was a world, my world, where I could be more than just a six-year-old neighborhood boy.

At six years old, I was a seasoned hunter of insects, my specialty – grasshoppers. I'd been catching these bugs since I was about three, the only three-year-old among a group of eight and nine-year-olds. But now I was the only hunter left. The eight and nine-year-olds were now ten and eleven-year-olds and hunting grasshoppers no longer held their interest; they had graduated to catching the snakes that populated the local creeks way beyond the boundaries of my mother's block. So, I was relegated to the empty lot. But that was fine with me. Who would want to catch stupid snakes anyway? They didn't even have legs.

I can still feel the heat of the sun kissing the nape of my neck as I crouched and made my way slowly through the tall weeds. My focus was keen, my senses on high alert. My eyes scanned the grass and weeds in search of my prey. I stepped carefully as I was intent on not giving my position away, and I had to avoid the sharp rocks that poked from the dark brown soil like broken bones of the earth. I also had to avoid the poison ivy: another case of that and my mother would really go on tilt. She had already cautioned me; the next step would be to restrict me from the empty lot. You see, after the first time I was exposed to the plant and broke out in a rash. I'd been warned repeatedly to avoid places where the plant grew. But how could I follow that rule when it would mean staying away from my hunting grounds? That would never do. After all, the empty lot was my own little savanna – and I was king.

Out of the corner of my eye, I saw movement. I froze as my eyes zeroed in on the target: a large brown grasshopper. Its skin provided camouflage so it blended with the brown of the dying weeds, making it invisible to the untrained eye. But, I was a veteran of the hunt; the camouflage was not enough to fool me. I inched closer, careful not to disturb the weeds, any slight movement and the grasshopper would jump away. I was getting closer, my movement undetected. Then I struck, with my right hand snapping out as quickly as the strike of a snake. I pulled my hand back, tufts of grass sticking out the sides. I could feel the insect frantically squirming, but there would be no escape from this prison.

I hurriedly navigated my way out of the weeds and entered my backyard. I picked up my grasshopper cage – an old pickle jar with holes poked through the lid. I unscrewed the top. This was the dangerous part – the transference of my prize to the pickle jar. I squinted my eyes. Every seasoned grasshopper hunter knew that they secreted this rusty colored liquid from their mouths -- we called it, spitting tobacco -- and if it got in your eyes, you could go blind. Quickly, I opened my hand and placed it on top of the jar dumping the tufts of grass and the grasshopper inside. I screwed the lid back on and held the jar towards the sun. I smiled as the grasshopper jumped repeatedly inside of its glass prison. After a few seconds, I placed the jar on the cement steps of my backyard and headed back to my hunting grounds. I had to catch another grasshopper. My prize needed a friend.

So, my little heart broke when I realized that my hunting grounds were being destroyed. There would be no more grasshopper hunting and, with that, an era was ending. I would no longer be a grasshopper hunter. As I watched the bulldozers dig up the earth, I made up my mind that day that I would no longer be held by the boundary of my mother's block. I had been a grasshopper hunter long enough; tomorrow I would begin a new era. I would sneak off the block and my old grasshopper cage would soon be filled with...snakes.

WHEN WE WERE CHILDREN

I

We were just children
in a land that ate
chocolate babies for breakfast.
I saw the best of us,
innocent, bright eyed and ready for the world
only to be consumed,
just a morsel
for the insatiable appetite of a beast.

We were just children:
our ideas about life
shaped by fantasies trapped in a box
where life's problems would fade away
'til the next episode;
but the reality would cause our feet to bleed
as the concrete cut our toes
through holes in our souls.

We were just children running up and down the block
shouting, "that's my car!"
We were nine-year-old explorers of the neighborhood
who could only see the fun we were having
but were blind to what was coming—
a perfect storm,
a deluge of decadence
with a surge of misery

that flooded our 'hoods
soaked the grounds of graveyards
and pounded
forty-foot high penitentiary walls.
How could we see?
We were just children
just children.

II

Acirema,
It was Oliver's pledge to you
that inspired a back door deal
with American spooks,
Islamic Revolutionaries and Contras.
Weapons flowed one way
and hostages flowed another
as the poor harvested snow
in the Columbian jungle.
Bricked up and shipped across freeways by Freeway
before anyone knew what was happening
a blizzard of pain
blanketed South Central
and the crack of a new era had dawned.

Acirema,
you promised us bliss packaged in a plastic vial
promoted as an escape from our collective misery.
but it was all a lie
We believed it would be fun
to play in the snow
'til vessels burst

and we could taste the blood in the drip;
'til we became transfixed by the reflection
on burnt glass of our own wide eyes staring back
as we became hypnotized by pale smoke—
which caused us to not give a fuck about
NOTHING!

Acirema why do you hate us so?
wasn't slavery enough,
lynching enough,
murder enough,
rape enough,
All we've ever done is love you
and you repay that love
with bullets ripping through flesh as
our hands are raised in surrender,
with brutal choke holds as we cry
"I can't breathe;"
with the murder of our children
as they play with toy guns:
with broken necks
in the back of police vans;
with executions for traffic violations.

Acirema, how long
do we have to shout
Black Lives Matter!
Til our voices are only
echoes of a tortured past
and our lives
only memories

like the *Arawak*—
who opened their arms to strangers
from the sea, only for
that kindness to be repaid
with murder, and enslavement,
their land and their future
snatched away,
regulating this proud and beautiful people
to just a footnote
in the history of conquest.

None of us are safe
we duck, we twerk,
we hide in skirts
or seek refuge in the false peace
of bottled water
that burns with the fire of self-destruction,
or fevered dreams
imagined along the route of bloody tracks
haunted by fiends.

Acirema, I hear your stomach rumbling
as you hunger for what our lives could be;
the doctor who cures cancer,
the lawyer who defends the poor,
the scientist who discovers
the key to eternal youth,
they've become lost
amongst the millions
that feed your appetite
as you grow fat from our potential.

Unrealized possibilities
that may never be
because you won't
stop feeding off your own.

III

To all who came before me
who sacrificed their lives for freedom
Now I know
that a free man
can never be a slave
and a slave can never be free
and those who couldn't feel
the weight of their shackles
was why, Ms. Tubman you had
to leave so many behind.

Now I know your heartbreak, Mr. Garvey,
as you tried to get us to
"know thy self"
and reclaim a glory long lost
only to be betrayed
by the very ones
you were trying to save.

Now I know
that the journey
from the wastelands of little
through the valley of X
and finally home to Shabazz

produced a man
unapologetic and fearless
in his struggle to
save those chocolate babies
from being devoured.

Now I know
that the preacher
who spoke truth to power
as he followed
a path of peace
would be ambushed
along the way
and as his friends
scanned the rooftops
following the trajectory
of the hate
that ended his life,
the inner cities
burst into flames
of despair and outrage.

Now I know
after black cats wearing black berets
stormed a Cali capital
they fathered an unwanted child—
and the state where
the earth shakes
gave birth to a new NRA
and its cries are the tools
we used to paint

our 'hoods crimson.

Now I know
that I too, was just a morsel
on the plate of a beast
that feasted off his abused children
an unhealthy diet that will kill him in the end—
but with his demise, everyone dies,
This I know…

THE HATE THAT HATE PRODUCED

A flash caught my eye as it burned through the fog of my codeine-induced haze. I turned to my right and squinted. He stood at the corner bus stop. He had on a white tank top that left the top of his chest and shoulders bare. A diamond encrusted chain stood out on his black skin like the Northern Lights in the Alaskan night skies, and every time he moved, the chain trapped the glow of the corner streetlight and sparkled. In an instant, I made a decision. I was taking that chain. In my mind, if I had that chain, its sparkle would blind people to my insecurities. I walked towards him, my stroll easy, as if I was just out for an evening walk. As I got closer, a hate-fueled anger began to build within me. *Who the fuck this black motherfucker think he is?* I wanted to hurt him. But, why? This man hadn't done anything to me. I continued slowly towards him and reached into my waistband to pull out my .38 revolver. I hid my gun behind my thigh; the metal of my weapon felt as cold as my beating heart.

He didn't notice me until I stood only a few feet behind him and I spoke, "Ay, yo, how long you been waiting?" He jumped, startled by my voice, and then he turned to face me. The roar of my gun discharging shattered the silence.

I jumped up, lost in blackness. Sweat-soaked sheets clung to my body. I shivered as my eyes adjusted to the dark. I lay on my back breathing rapidly, staring into nothingness. My heart rate began to slow down. But then my mind replayed the disturbing image of the dream. A face frozen in shock filled the blackness. My heart began to race again. I was panicking, frightened by what I remembered. The face of this man, murdered in my dream by my own hand, was a familiar one – it was my own.

As I lay on my flat, hard mattress, staring into the darkness, this dream kept playing in my mind. What did it mean? Why was I trying to kill myself? Wide awake now, my mind was in overdrive, trying to interpret the vagueness of my sub consciousness. Was I depressed? After all, I was in the twenty-third year of a life-without-parole prison sentence. Maybe the hopelessness of that circumstance had finally overwhelmed me. But no, it couldn't be that. I loved life too much. The fight to be free gave my life meaning. As a result of my circumstance, I had become a man with a spark within him that burned bright, casting off any shadows of hopelessness that an incarcerated existence could create. So, this dream had to be caused by something else.

As the hours of the night slowly ticked by, I was nearly at my wits' end and I had almost given up trying to figure it out. But then, a thought slowly began to reveal itself. I reached deep into the recesses of my mind to give this thought shape and suddenly everything became clear. There was a sickness imbedded deep within my psyche that was the driving force behind everything I did. I had become my own personal angel of death, subconsciously determined to destroy myself. This realization took me back to my earliest memories when I was first exposed to this "infection." I was able to see how this affliction progressed and how it determined the path my life would take.

I was born in a place where row homes lined both sides of the street. It was a blue-collar working town where African American, Hispanic, Italian, and Irish lived in their own little enclaves… separated, not by law, but by the comfort that comes with people who share cultural and family ties. There was warmth about my old neighborhood, a love, a spirit of community that touched everyone and everything. You could smell it in the sweet aroma of barbecue sauce that drifted from the grills on sidewalks during summertime block parties. You could hear it in the laughter of the children who played up and down the blocks: little boys would be playing basketball, using plastic milk crates nailed to telephone poles as basketball rims. The games would be highly competitive and trash-talking would sometimes get out of hand, but the spirit of community had a strong presence, so all would be forgiven and the games would continue. The little girls, it seemed, never argued. They would jump rope, play hopscotch and run from the boys, who chased them for kisses. I grew up in a place where cheesesteaks and hoagie shops, soft pretzel and hot dog vendors filled the broad avenues.

On the surface, all would seem to be well, but hidden from the naked eye was a sickness that was so infectious that it contaminated the very foundation of my childhood home. This place where I grew up was America's fifth largest city,

Philadelphia, Pennsylvania, ironically nicknamed The City of Brotherly Love.

I was raised in the decade of the 70's, right after the Civil Rights struggle and during the height of the Black Power Movement. It was a time when the Afro had replaced the chemically burned-out straight-hair style of the process and the people wore Kente' cloth Dashikis in an effort to reclaim a long lost African heritage. On hot summer days, James Brown's soulful voice could be heard blasting from radios throughout the black communities. His hit song, *Say It Loud, I'm Black and I'm Proud,* was the anthem of the time and the black fist raised to the sky in defiance was the symbol.

This period of racial pride and activism didn't last very long, though. Maybe it was short-lived because, at this time Frank Rizzo was the police commissioner and his gestapo-like police force stepped up their brutal police tactics. Not a day passed by without the police reminding black men of their "niggerness" with the violent swings of nigger-beaters and the contrasting colors of blood red flowing down black skin. Or maybe it was because of the assassinations and imprisonment of countless Black Power Movement leaders. Or maybe it was the simple fact that white superiority was centuries in the making and one movement over a few short years wasn't enough to overcome all the psychological damage that had been done.

Although it was only a short period of time, I could witness this surge in racial pride, but it didn't influence me. It was as if the movement had forgotten its children. Our parents were so caught up in the struggle against police brutality and the fight for equality that they neglected to protect the minds of the children. We were vulnerable, unable to guard against the legacy of our tortured past that taught us that black skin was a curse. So, while the adults battled to be free from the shackles of oppression, they were outflanked and in the process, they lost the children as the movement faded to black.

As a result, we saw ourselves through a lens tinted by a plantation ideology that taught us that to be black was to be insignificant – marginalized, almost invisible. This idea was implemented centuries ago by the flesh ripping lash of a slave master's whip. It was maintained by a segment of the white population who hid under white hoods and brutally instilled this concept, through a campaign of terror where lynchings, rapes and even murder were the means. It was adopted by a black population who, because of the fear that these terror campaigns instilled, accepted this belief about themselves.

It was an idea that was fostered through religion by ministers standing behind pulpits with all their self-righteous indignation. Their voices would thunder in churches across the country as they preached about a European God and the cursed African descendants of Ham. It was an ideology that was nurtured through history books that relegated the African American experience to a few short paragraphs. It was sustained by images of black people broadcasted to the world as gangbangers, pimps, thugs, drug dealers, convicts, prostitutes, and nannies. All these things were continuously reinforced even through the language we spoke: black deeds, black thoughts, black ball, and black Friday. Because of this, we internalized the message that black was inferior. So, although the Black Power Movement had the adults bursting with pride, it was a short burst, because before anyone knew what was happening *Super Fly* had become the theme of the times and the hypodermic needle had become the symbol.

I can remember that, during my formative years, to be black was not something to say loud and proud. For me, my blackness and anything remotely African was my shame. I hated to watch my little sister cry because my mother combed her hair out in an Afro before school. I can remember thinking: *Why can't she make her hair straight and pretty like the other little girls?*

I can recall being chased by the boogey man of my blackness, hounded by my dark skin. I would search high and low for an avenue of escape that was as hard to find as the shadow of the moon. My ebony skin tone was a coat of shame that I couldn't take off. Like a vampire, I avoided the sunlight, not because I would burn, but because I didn't want to get darker. I wasn't the only child affected by this shame. The other children expressed their shame through an unmerciful mockery of my blackness. "He cute to be so black." "We all black, just not as black as you." "Tar baby." "There go black Rell." "Blackie." "Ay, Terrell, if you lay in the street you'll turn invisible." "Casper the burnt ghost." These were just a few of the names and jokes that demonstrated the self-hate that infected us all

I was constantly aware of my African heritage. It hung heavy on my shoulder like a yoke, a punishment that I couldn't avoid. Everywhere I looked, I was taught my complexion was ugly. It was bad, evil. The bad guys wore black hats and rode black horses. Tarzan was my hero and I can remember imagining my room to be an African jungle where I could imitate his call and swing from make-believe vines made up of bed sheets tied to the top bunk. Powerful and white, I would be the hero who saved the fair-skinned Jane from the black savage hordes. *Little Black Sambo* was one of the books we read in elementary school. I would shrink in my seat and try to disappear when I would hear the hushed giggles and whispered comparisons of this character to myself and the other dark-skinned children.

The politics of race was a lesson not learned, but absorbed into my psyche. It became a part of me, affecting my worldview; it was even in the songs the little girls sang at recess time: "If you're light, you're alright. If you're black, step back." My childhood was one filled with the legacy of the enslaved. It was an infection of the mind that destroyed my self-esteem. I became the boy who subconsciously turned on himself. I replaced the iron chains of my ancestors with gold ones that hung heavy with the weight of my rejected identity. My new slave master became Gucci and Cartier. The overseer was the alcohol that dulled the pain of being me. His whip was the codeine-laced syrup that intoxicated my mind and helped me to forget. The cotton fields were the streets where I toiled from sun up 'til sundown, becoming schooled in the art of my own self-destruction. By the time I had reached adulthood, I was a full-fledged enemy of myself and of anyone who resembled me.

The self-hate that I suffered from fed on my soul for most of my life. Like a malignant tumor, it spread through my body. I was diseased, the sickness of self-loathing dictating my every action.

No surprise then that I find myself here, wrapped in sweat-soaked sheets in a small cramped cell where I had suddenly, inexplicably ended up the antagonist in my own life story, dreaming of becoming my own executioner...

LET THE FIRE BURN

For my man Mike Africa

In '85 I was
a sixteen-year-old man-child
who knew everything
about nothing.
My life was about a party,
How much money I could get,
How fly I could be,
And how many different places
I could plant my seed.
But then the earth shook
beneath my feet and I can remember
when my homie Ahm said,
"Yo, they just dropped a bomb on Move!
and now they're just letting the fire burn."

Bullets blocked all the exits
but Ramona ducked, dodged and
tossed a little Birdy to safety
while the rest burned alive.
Their cries were incinerated in the inferno
as the reflection of the flames
danced on the black barrels
of guns.
And all they did was watch
as the fire burned.

A little white lie cloaked in blue

tarnished a golden shield
and grew so large
it separated us from them
and it became easy
to just want them gone
after all, their hair was too nappy, too long
the way they lived, too dirty, too raw.
The acceptance of white superiority was the rent,
and payment was long overdue.
But since when do you serve
an eviction with a bomb?
Only when it's time
to let the fire burn.

The roar of the blaze
was the beat of the flame
as the fire did the wobble
up and down Osage.
Grey smoke tinted crimson
with the blood of Africa
blocked out the sun
and a misty haze
fell from the heavens
as God shed tears
for the innocent.
But those tears
weren't enough to extinguish
the centuries of hate
that burned within
the windows of an ice-cold blue expanse.
On a West Philly rooftop

an explosion shook the city,
and lives that have always been
considered CHEAP
couldn't purchase any mercy
'cause the price of humanity
cost too much...
So nothing was done and the fire just burned.

The dawn saw pale smoke
that chauffeured the spirits
of the dead
through updrafts of heat—
an escape route from the hell
of a city block ablaze.
Broken bones of burnt homes
was all that was left
but nothing could erase
the horror of what we saw
as we all stood by and watched
as they let the fire burn.

Lynching jumped off the pages of history
and set up shop on a West Philly block.
and all I did was watch—
while my naiveté died in the flames
when they let the fire burn.

GAUNTLET OF

HATE

It was an hour past dawn and the sun a freshly cut diamond, hung like a pendent against the blue sky. Its light added a warmth and radiance to the day despite winter's relentless approach. The leaves understood that the life sustaining warmth of the summer months were slipping away, so they prepared for the inevitable: their descent. Desperately clinging to their perches on the brown, gnarled branches of trees, they transformed into their bright colors, precursors of their death. One by one, their tenuous hold on life faded, their grips failed, and they abandoned their perch on the trees as they floated inexorably to the hard concrete.

This was America in 1979 during the Iran hostage crisis. News coverage of blindfolded Americans, their faces haggard and their clothes disheveled was broadcast on millions of television sets across the country. Jimmy Carter's presidency was reeling as the top-dog status of America took a hit. It was at the height of the OPEC oil embargo, which affected rich and poor alike. The public was in a panic as the price of gas and gas tank locks exploded. Sleek, bright red Corvettes, blue Impalas, yellow Trans Am and white Mustangs; hulking Buick Electra 225s (better known in the hood as the *Deuce and A Quarter*), blood red Cadillacs and blue collar pick-up trucks stretched for blocks in long gas lines.

Bigger was better, then. Fuel efficiency had yet to become a part of the national consciousness. This was the America where manufacturing was still king and Detroit was still the car capital of the world. The Japanese economic recovery had yet to be completed, and the subsequent invasion of the fuel-efficient compact cars of Honda and Toyota were still off in the not-so-distant future.

Two-story row homes, identical and packed together, decorated the Philadelphia streets. Empty lots, filled with weeds, rusted bicycle parts and worn out couches, could be found scattered throughout the neighborhoods. Abandoned homes, graffiti-smeared boards covering the broken windows and doors, were interspersed among the row homes like sores that couldn't heal. 7-Elevens, Mom & Pop corner stores that sold everything from cheesesteaks to mop heads were minutes away from every home. Bars, Delis and State Stores, staked out by the neighborhood winos, also provided people with an alcohol-fueled escape from the struggle of being poor. A thick canopy of trees provided camouflage for the fields of overgrown grass, broken glass-covered concrete walkways, worn-out, rusted, broken-down swings, sliding boards, and dilapidated basketball courts of inner city playgrounds. Block after block was the same. So, what was it that divided one poor neighborhood from the next?

If you could somehow transport yourself back in time to 1979 and witness a little yellow school bus cross this divide, you wouldn't be able to make the distinction between one poor neighborhood and another. But if you were on that bus, you would know. A strange sense of foreboding would subtly creep into your being. Did something smell different? Did the temperature change? No, it was undetectable by normal human senses. It was an invasion of the subconscious, like a demonic possession of the soul. It was a metaphysical thing, as if ghosts from our tortured past cried out in warning and spoke, not with words, but with a centuries-old tension. This foreboding enveloped our little yellow school bus like a thick fog as it transported a fresh crop of fifth graders on their first day of school into a neighborhood that looked exactly like ours but, as we would regrettably find out, was not.

A hush fell over us all as we entered this strange new world. It was as if we all had developed a sixth sense about what was going to happen next. To this day, I can't understand how a group of ten-year-olds, their lives not yet tainted by the hatred, bigotry and cruelty of the world could feel this tension, but we all could sense it. Maybe it was a sensation given off by the driver and chaperone, the only adults on the bus who had been making this trip for the past couple years. Or maybe it was an organic thing born only in America, where white superiority is the father of all racial conflict.

An America where little black girls and boys in their bright white Sunday dresses and black Sunday suits, surrounded by armed Federal Marshals, were ushered through a mob of angry pale faces. Shouts of "NIGGER GO HOME!" deafened them. Spit from the mouths of men, women and children, splattered across their faces. They were terrified. No sudden movement; they kept their arms glued to their sides, so the spit ran slowly, agonizingly down their faces. Eyes downcast, they were marched into this bedlam of hostility. Brown vs. Board of Education had just been ruled upon, and these children were one of the first groups of students to desegregate the all-white schools.

That was the south in the 1950's and maybe, two decades later, the scar of the Civil Rights struggle was still bleeding, or the wound was left untreated north of the Mason Dixon Line. Whatever it was, I felt it as the bus rumbled under the electric trolley lines of Wyoming Avenue. It was as if invisible hands gripped my young soul and squeezed tight. My heart began to pound and my throat became dry. At the time, I thought the uneasiness was just the anxiety of attending a new school. I turned to look at my friends, wondering if they felt the same as I. What I know now, that I didn't know then, was beneath the smiles and laughter, there was an uneasiness that settled over us all that was bigger, much bigger, then that first-day-at-a-new-school feeling.

The impact of the first rock smashing against the side of the bus startled us, but we weren't afraid, at least not yet. We were just curious as children always are. What was that sound? Did we hit a dog? We all looked out the windows. That was when we saw them. Cloaked in green army fatigue jackets, faded wrangler jeans and canvas Converse sneakers, bearded white men stood on both sides of the street. Their faces were beet-red from the cold and the exertion of their facial muscles that held hate-fueled scowls. The chaperones put on brave faces, but their wide-eyed, panicked glances and the slight quiver in their voices betrayed them. These clues allowed the fear to become infectious and like a virus, it contaminated us all.

I watched the rock as it left his hand, my eyes following it as it sped towards us. Right before it made impact, I closed my eyes and ducked. Then I heard the shouts, "GET THE NIGGERS" "WE DON'T WANT YOU HERE NIGGERS!" A fist-sized rock smashed against the side of the bus and terror was born. Its hunger devoured us like wolves among sheep and we could feel its teeth penetrate our hearts. Another rock smashed against the side of the bus and the floodgates of hate burst wide open.

"FUCKING NIGGERS! YOU BLACK MONKEYS! GET OUT OF OUR NEIGHBORHOOD!" As the rocks smashed against the bus, the noise terrified us. However, that was only noise. It was the shouts of, "KILL THE NIGGERS!" that struck deep. These verbal assaults were personal; they were talking about us. Those words were so powerful – they instilled a fear that would turn our dreams into nightmares.

My friend Tonya's scream sliced through the chaos of shouts, cries and sobs as white men, their faces stained with murderous intent, leapt onto the back of the bus and began yanking on the emergency doors. I felt trapped, buried alive by an avalanche of hate. There was nowhere for me to run, nowhere to hide. "Please, God, don't let 'em break the doors open. Please make 'em go away." I whispered.

I guess the God that I prayed to that September morning couldn't hear my prayers, maybe the shouts of, "WE DON'T WANT YOU HERE NIGGERS!" were too loud, because they continued to throw rocks, and they continued to shout racial slurs. I clenched my little fist. At that point, I was resolved to fight. What choice did I have? I never thought about the police coming to the rescue. Instead I thought about my father, I thought about my seven uncles, and I felt a spark of anger. *They wouldn't dare do this if they were here.* Another crash: "FUCKING NIGGERS!" Another hate-filled shout and my short-lived bravado faded like the whimpering of my friends who sat paralyzed with fright, huddled in the high back seat of the school bus. This gauntlet of hate lasted only for the length of a city block, about sixty seconds. But for us, the children, it lasted a lifetime.

Later as I sat in my all-white classroom and we were asked to stand and salute the flag, I remained seated. I watched as my classmates recited those hollow words. *"I PLEDGE OF ALLEGIANCE TO THE FLAG..."* On a chilly autumn morning, a bus full of ten-year-olds went through an initiation... *"OF THE UNITED STATES OF AMERICA..."* In order for us to truly understand what it meant to be black in America, we had to go through this gang rite... *"AND TO THE REPUBLIC..."* this kangaroo line of terror... *"FOR WHICH IT STANDS..."* and once we emerged—innocence gone... *"ONE NATION..."* in our eyes... *"UNDER*

GOD..." America would never be the same again... *"INDIVISIBLE..."* In a matter of seconds... *"WITH LIBERTY..."* The pledge... *"AND JUSTICE..."* became a blur of background noise... *"FOR ALL..."* My mind became filled with images of red-faced white men, their eyes cold, and their mouths hurling the word *"NIGGER!"* Like a rock that smashed against my soul. All my romantic ideals of white picket fences, polite people, baseball and apple pie were shattered that day. As my classmates recited the pledge of allegiance, all I could think about was that GAUNTLET OF HATE, scared to death that it would still be there at 3 o'clock.

THE GAME

In the beginning
the game was something
played for fun
1-2-3 red light,
Hide & Seek,
and Freeze Tag
made the summer months
the best months.
Tar stained the knees
of faded jeans
and filled the plastic bottle milk tops,
as the heat of the summertime
sun baked the napes of necks,
but the game continued on; the heat
was paid no mind
as milk tops
were plucked
across the smooth black street
inside a painted square
trying to avoid the dead man.
Catch a girl/get a girl

was a favorite at recess time
Yeah…the little girls
were fast
but the boys
were a little faster
as colorful summer dresses
fluttering in their wake became
closer.

The rubber soles
of Converse sneakers
kicked up diamond chips
from broken soda bottles
until the whistle blew
and the game, the game, yeah, the game
well…the game would resume again tomorrow.
In the beginning
the game was something
played, no stakes
it was just for fun.

As the glass bottle spun
upon the concrete stoop
codeine coursed through
blood streams,
and all of a sudden
the game, the game, yeah, the game

wasn't fun anymore.
Somehow along the way blood stained
a police-taped square
and the dead man
became something unavoidable
because the game... by then
was played for keeps;
to live – not hide
to die – not seek.
The little boys
weren't so little anymore
but they were still fast –
not to catch a girl,
But...
to hurdle a forty-foot wall,
careful
on the way over
'cause
the razor wire
cuts deep...

"Terrell! Get out here now!'

I had been out late like I was every night – at work – at least that's what my father and stepmother believed: that I was hard at work on the graveyard shift cleaning office buildings in downtown Washington, DC. I was hard at work all right, but it was far from downtown and it had nothing to do with cleaning. As a matter of fact, I only worked five minutes away at the Fort Totten Apartment Complex. If only my father and stepmother really knew what my so-called work was, there would be no way that I would have been allowed to live in their home. You see, my father and stepmother were drug counselors and I was the neighborhood drug dealer. Kind of ironic, right? I can remember justifying my actions by saying, "Shit, if not for people like me, my parents would be out of work." The mind of a twenty-year-old in all of its brilliance.

So, after a long night of haggling with crack-heads over cocaine prices, smoking blunts and drinking forties, I was in one of those alcohol hungover, coma-like slumbers. I actually thought I was dreaming the first time I heard my stepmother holler out my name. But by the fourth time, I knew it wasn't a dream.

Damn. I rolled over and put the pillow over my head in hopes that she would give up and just wait until I got up on my own.

"Terrell!" I could tell by the high pitched and almost guttural shout that echoed off the apartment walls that her waiting for me to get up on my own was not going to happen. I could also tell by the force of her tone that something wasn't right and it was probably my fault.

Knowing her next move would be to march in my room and snatch the covers off, I forced myself up. Half asleep, I stumbled into the living room.

As soon as I entered, the first thing I noticed was my stepmother sitting on the couch, her face drawn tight in an angry scowl. She was holding something in her hand. Looking me dead in the eye, she lifted her hand up.

"What is this?" She held a pair of white panties in her hand.

"Panties." I responded, now clearly agitated that I had been awakened about something I had nothing to do with.

"What did I tell you about having sex in my house?"

"Huh?" I was confused. What did these strange panties have to do with me having sex? "What are you talking about? I ain't got nothing to do with those panties."

My stepmother exploded. I would have never thought that my stepmother used the language that erupted from her mouth, and it shocked me.

My stepmother wasn't this evil woman bent on making my life miserable. There was an incident that took place previously that had given her plenty of reason to react the way that she did. A couple months prior, the family genius, which would be me, decided to take my father's advice. I was a young man prone to making bone-headed decisions; I guess that's why I became a drug dealer. My father, very aware of the poor choices young men make, was constantly in my ear. He was always sharing stories of the lessons he learned in his critical transition from adolescence to manhood. Problem was, I thought he was out of touch. In my mind, the things he went through in the 50's just didn't apply in the 80's. So, for the most part, his advice went unheeded.

My father was an avid reader and he loved to write. He said to me one day, "Terrell, you need to write. Writing can be therapeutic, it can be liberating. It can help you gain some direction in life. I've kept a journal since I was about sixteen and it has helped me tremendously. You should try it, son."

I took this advice. But now that I think back on it, it was really a perversion of advice taking. I didn't start a journal because I thought it was liberating, therapeutic or a good way of providing some direction in my life. The only reason I started this journal was to keep track of all my sexual exploits while spending time in the Chocolate City.

Now, I could lie and say that I had a notebook full of stuff, but I didn't. It was just a page and a half of the most graphic description of one incident. After one of my blunt smoking, Cisco drinking nights, I had an intoxicated inspiration to add to my journal. I can't remember if I actually added to it or not. All I know is that I forgot to put the journal away. I left it out on my dresser drawer where my inquisitive ten-year-old sister found it, read it, and promptly took it to my stepmother.

This was why my stepmother was so upset about the panties; I had exposed her daughter to some very disturbing and graphic language. So, now I stood in the middle of the front room as my stepmother berated me. I was disrespectful, an ingrate, a pig, nasty and a whole bunch of other names that are just too vile to repeat. Of course, I tried to defend myself. Nothing feels worse than being accused of something you didn't do. I was angry, but nothing I said could prove my innocence; after all, the evidence pointed to me. She had my history of transgressions and the panties, which, together, equaled my guilt.

I became the "panty bandit," which meant extra scrutiny if I invited a female friend over to hang out, and absolutely no female friends were allowed in the house if no one was home.

It remained that way the whole year that I was out there visiting my father. It wasn't until a few years later that I learned that my stepmother found out that I was telling the truth about those panties. Did I get an apology? No. She never even mentioned the incident again. I found out by accident through a conversation I had with another one of my sisters. We were reminiscing about my visit to DC and I mentioned the panty incident. My sister laughed and said, "Terrell, Ma Raine knew that you ain't have nothing to do with that. About a week after she confronted you, she told me about the incident and how she cussed you out, and then she showed me the panties. I said to her, 'Ma Raine, those panties are mine'."

My stepmother and I never talked about the conversation she had with my sister. To this day, I sometimes wonder what went through her mind when she found out I was telling the truth. I would like to imagine that she felt terrible for not believing me. But even if she didn't, a small part of me felt satisfied that at least she discovered that I was innocent.

IN-XILE

THE PRISON OF MY MIND

You know that feeling you get when you're watching a movie and the scene shifts to a city block and the background music kicks in, suggesting the hero is getting ready to die? Well, that's how Ludlow Street was in the evening hours. Broken bottles and trash littered the pavement, only a couple of street lamps were working, leaving some areas in complete darkness. There were no homes, just the back entrances to businesses and abandoned factories. The only traffic was me—a twelve-year-old on the way home from a friend's house.

Although it looked foreboding, for me it was my home, my hood, and I had no fear. To walk alone down this dark street was as normal to me as a stroll through a city park.

Midway through the block, a lone figure approached. Nothing to be alarmed about... I probably knew him. By the time, I realized that wasn't the case, he was only a few feet away. But it was cool, still no reason to be alarmed. Then I looked into his eyes. He gave me a cold stare as if he hated me. His eyebrows were bunched together and his lips were twisted into a grimace of pure malice. But how could this be? He had to be about eighteen years old, which was way beyond the age range of anyone I hung out with and I'd never seen him before. He sneered, reached into his waistline and pulled out a small, chrome automatic pistol.

To my twelve-year-old eyes, the hole in the barrel of that gun looked as huge as the black hole in the center of the Milky Way. My fear amplified this vacuum, and I became lost, as my senses focused on that hole. I was numb. I could hear no sounds and the night became darker as if the only street lamps that were working had burned out. But it was just my fear swallowing me into the black space of the barrel of that gun.

I could feel my heart pounding against my rib cage. I started to cry. But to the teenager who held that gun in my face, my tears meant nothing. "Take that fucking jacket off!" he barked.

My sobs broke the silence of that summer evening in hopes that my tears would buy me some mercy. But my tears weren't enough. The only thing they could buy was a smirk and a louder demand. "Shut the fuck up and take that jacket off!"

In 1981, for the young people who lived in the City of Brotherly Love, my jacket – a Members Only – was the shit. It had taken me months of packing and carrying bags at the corner supermarket to save enough money to buy one. Now in only a microsecond of that time, my jacket was taken from me, all my hard work to benefit someone else. I was reluctant to give it up. But was it worth my life? What if I refuse and he shoots me? In a flash, all my options were weighed and my life tipped the scales.

Slowly, I removed my Members Only jacket. My hand shook and my body quaked from my sobs. The teenage boy snatched my jacket from my hand. "You got some money on you, chump?" His voice was as cold as his stare. He began patting my pockets.

Hypnotized by the gun, my humiliation and helplessness had no time to register. All I could think of was getting out of that situation unharmed.

"Punk motherfucker," he hissed.

His palm against my face was the next sensation that I felt. It's funny how, when remembering life-changing events, the most insignificant things stick out in your mind. Like, right before he shoved me, I can recall how his hand smelled like chicken grease. As he shoved me backwards, I stumbled and crashed to the ground, slamming my head against the concrete. Blue pinpoints of light danced in my vision as I lay on my back. I could hear the teenager's rubber-soled sneakers pounding on the ground as he took off running. But I remained on the ground, too scared to move.

Like a goldfish swimming in a tank full of barracudas, I was overcome by a feeling of extreme helplessness. This wasn't the first time I had experienced this feeling. But it was the first time I felt like this in my own neighborhood. If I couldn't feel safe in my own hood, then I couldn't feel safe anywhere. Who would want to live a life where you were always afraid? Not me. It was at that moment, my twelve-year-old self made a vow that would change my life forever. I would never be a victim again. I would be the victimizer. I picked myself up from the ground, brushed myself off, wiped away my tears and walked home, leaving my innocence behind. The goldfish swimming with the barracudas grew some teeth that day. If I could help it, I would never feel that helpless again.

That summer night cost me more than my pride and a Members Only jacket. It also cost me my freedom. I took myself to trial as I lay on my back blinking at those blue pinpoints of light. I found myself guilty of weakness and fear and I sentenced myself to a life of thuggery. There would be no escape, no parole from this mental incarceration: the stone walls stretched to infinity and the steel bars were unbreakable. I became a prisoner to circumstance and my fear was the guard who held the keys. At twelve years old, my socialization began. Brick by brick, I restricted myself, killing my potential in the process. My freedom was taken from me that night and my mind became my prison.

There's a ghost in my life that's been around for as long as I can remember. Whenever I look into the mirror, he's there. I can see him in the shape of my eyes, the tone of my skin, the color of my hair and the way I smile. I can hear him when I speak, as his words become my words. This ghost is my father. When he was alive, he was barely around, so to me he was like a spirit, his presence hovering just outside my consciousness.

My earliest memory of being aware that I had a father was when I was about five years old. He lived in Washington D.C. while my mother and I lived in Philly. I can remember looking in my mother's soft brown eyes and asking her, "Mommy, where's my father?" I can't remember my mother's response, but I do recall the first time I met him, when the ghostly image of the man became flesh and bone: tall, dark, with brown eyes just like my own, a warm and endearing smile and strong arms that picked me up and held me close. But what stands out to me more than anything else about that day was this feeling of apprehension that made me shy away. I was afraid of this man whose blood pumps through my veins and whose face I inherited. But, why? Maybe it was because he was a stranger and I reacted the same way that most children do when they encounter people they don't know. For most children, that kind of fear lasts for only a short period of time, while mine was a presence that haunted me for decades. Maybe it was because I was used to my mother and he was a man—strong, intimidating, his voice deep, like a distant thunderclap. Whatever the reason, I was torn between wanting to love him and being afraid of him.

Throughout my life, I only spent brief periods with my father. This built a wall between us. And the estrangement was the mortar that held the wall together. Every year that passed and the older I got, the more bricks were added. There was no schedule of visits that I could look forward to, like every summer or every other weekend. They were sporadic, unexpected and most times unwanted, like the time he popped up at my mother's house on a quick stop-over as he traveled back to DC from Newark, New Jersey.

I was twelve years old. It was a late Sunday afternoon and I was just about to head out to the corner store with a pocket full of quarters. I was excited. It was time for my daily battle defending the earth, playing my favorite game, *Space Invaders*. The front door to my mother's house opened and my father strolled in as if he owned it. I was surprised to see him and a little upset because my afternoon plans were ruined. As soon as my father saw me, a smile lit his face, his teeth ivory white, contrasted sharply with his dark skin tone. As he opened his arms wide and embraced me, the scent of him immediately drifted up my nose—cigarette smoke mingled with cheap cologne. Oh, how I hated that smell. I crinkled my nose and began to breathe through my mouth. My father then took a seat on the couch. He patted the spot next to him and I reluctantly sat down. There was an awkward silence, followed by that old parental cliché.

"So, son, what do you want to be when you grow up?"

I thought I would impress him when I replied, "I want to fly fighter jets."

My father looked at me and I watched full of disappointment, as his smile evaporated.

"Terrell, why would you want to kill other black people?"

At the time, I knew nothing of racial politics or American Imperialism—its obsession to dominate the world and its resources at the expense of poor people's lives. All I knew was that I wanted to be an American hero, to protect the world from the hordes of space invaders… and my father was disappointed with my choice. Tears threatened to leak from my eyes as I withdrew from him even more. I retreated further behind my wall. From that one rejection, I felt like nothing I chose as a career path would be good enough. My dreams of the future became deferred that day as I resigned myself to thinking of only the present.

It would be a few more years before I saw my father again. I was fifteen and too much for my mother to handle. I wanted to stay out late, smoke weed, drink alcohol and syrup, and pop pills. I was already a father, and school became just a place to pick up girls. My mother was fed up, so she decided to send me to stay with him one summer in hopes that he would straighten me out.

Phyllis Hyman's angelic voice singing about a meeting on the moon flowed softly through my father's car speakers. We were at a red light. Sunlight peeked through the tree canopy on New Hampshire Avenue in Northwest Washington, DC, slicing through the shade and creating small spotlights on the black asphalt. I could feel his eyes burning a hole through the side of my head right before he spoke.

"Terrell, you see those young brothers standing on the corner?"

I peeked into the eyes of this older version of myself and quickly turned away. My apprehension wouldn't allow me to hold his gaze. I nodded my head in response, but kept my eyes glued in front of me.

"Well, you can leave this town and come back twenty years from now and those brothers will still be on that same corner doing the same stuff."

"Come on, dad, how you know that? What, you can tell the future now?"

"I don't have to able to read the future to predict how their lives will turn out. You see, a lot of black men get to a certain age—about seventeen—and they stop growing mentally. So, what you have as a result of that are men with the mental capacity of children. They're stuck, stagnant in their development. That's why those brothers will always be on that corner, stuck at seventeen, doing what seventeen-year-olds do."

I was quietly listening to what my father said, but at the same time thinking, *damn, here he go with this lecturing shit.* I was a fifteen-year-old man child who knew everything about nothing, and the last person I wanted to have a conversation with was my father.

Almost two decades later, bombs dropped over Iraq and Afghanistan as fighter jets with the stars and stripes painted on their wings roared overhead. Hundreds of thousands of men, women, and children's lives were snuffed out as America flexed its muscle. I felt saddened as I watched my television screen fill up with the grainy, eerie, and green of night vision cameras, thousands of tracer rounds and bright explosions that lit up the skies like fireworks.

My father's words echoed in my mind. I thought of the lesson he was trying to teach me all those years ago when he killed my dreams of flying fighter jets. I finally understood. There were no space invaders, just the slaughter of innocents, and there is no heroism in that. If not for my father expressing his disappointment in my career choice, that could've been me piloting those flying machines of death, soaking my hands in the blood of thousands. I was grateful, but I couldn't thank him because I had retreated behind a wall that had become too high to climb.

I didn't appreciate what my father said during that car ride until years later. I found myself stuck behind a real wall surrounded by men who dreamt of being rap stars. The problem was that they were in their forties. It was frustrating for me because I couldn't escape and I was engulfed by conversations that never went beyond sports, sex, fashionable clothing, expensive jewelry, and fly cars. I felt stifled by the acceptance of ignorance as cool. I was surrounded by people who had no aspirations to be more than thugs, drugs dealers, or killers, and I couldn't understand why.

But then one day, Phyllis Hyman's *Meet Me On The Moon* came on the radio and it took me back to that car ride. It was then that I finally understood what my father was trying to tell me all those years ago. What he said then, was true at that moment and I could see it all around me. I wished I could tell him how right he was, but he had already passed on.

My father has been gone now for over ten years. He passed away just when the wall of my fear began to crumble. As the cloud of dust settles, I'm left standing among the stones of regret with the last brick of apprehension in my hand. Tears leave trails through the dust that covered my face as I think about the cruelty of it all. All my life I've been afraid of this man and as soon as I was able to conquer that fear—he was gone. Grief fills my soul as memories of him flow through my mind.

I love my father, and this love has always been with me, even when I was afraid. While he was alive, this feeling was the ghost haunting the edges of my consciousness. It kept him with me even though he was absent most of the time.

After my father passed on, this love became the spirit breathing life back into my past, keeping his words with me to guide me as I continue along the path of my life.

TO CATCH

A SHADOW

I would awaken to blackness. It would be the middle of the night. Like dragonflies, my eyes would dart back and forth – where am I? Instinctively I would reach out and feel for her; she wouldn't be there, just empty space. Then it would dawn on me, I wasn't home, my wife wouldn't be here – shit, I'm still in prison. I would blink rapidly as my eyes adjusted to the darkness. What time is it? I would turn on my TV to check the time: 3:30 am, just like I thought.

Like an organic alarm clock, a dream had awakened me. It was the same dream, day in, day out and, without fail, it awakened me at 3:30 am. In this dream, I would be driving. I would pick up my cell phone, one of those big bulky ones from the early nineties with the carrying case and the shoulder strap. I would dial her number, and the phone would just keep on ringing. Where the fuck is my wife? I would keep calling and she would never answer the phone. But then, my dream would shift and I would go from calling her to actually being with her.

We would be in the house, sitting at the dinner table. The flickering glow of candle flames would leave dancing shadows on the walls. The room would be cast in romantic dimness and the faint aroma of jasmine would linger in the air. Maxwell's smooth tenor, singing about a fistful of tears, could be heard pumping softly through the speakers located strategically around the room for maximum sound effect.

There would be no one there but her and me. I would be talking, I think she would be listening, but I'm not sure, for she wouldn't be facing me.

But then something I said would cause her to look my way. Butterflies would explode into flight in the pit of my gut and my heart would pick up the cadence of a marching band's drum line. I would feel an urgency that would intensify by the second. I would be staring at the woman I love, but I wouldn't be able to see her face. Why couldn't I see those naturally arched eyebrows that gave her such a serious look? Why couldn't I see those dark browns that sparkled every time she smiled? Why couldn't I see the jet-black hair that contrasted with and framed her light skin? Why couldn't I see the infectious smile? It would be as if she was a reflection of everyone and no one. I'm desperate. Why couldn't I see her face?

In this dream, I would muster all my mental strength to conjure up her beautiful image, but it would be to no avail, she would remain faceless. I would awaken to blackness with my breath coming in gasps, the pressure of four walls would be closing in on me and there would be nowhere for me to go.

My heart would still be pounding and my whole being would be engulfed by extreme vulnerabilities: does she really love me? Will she abandon me? Is she with someone else? I would clench my fist and pound on my flat, hard jailhouse mattress in anger and frustration. I hate to feel that way, trapped by the circumstances of forty-foot walls, watchtowers, rifles, razor wire, being powerless and at the mercy of strangers who judge me without knowing me. To love and be loved while serving time is an elusive thing, almost impossible to attain, like trying to catch a shadow. It will be under a constant assault, sabotaged by forces you have no control over.

"BZ-5409, you have a visit!" When the correctional officer announced this over the intercom system, for me, Christmas had arrived early. Like a child who goes to sleep with dreams of presents in the morning, I was filled with a joyful anticipation. In a few moments, I would no longer be separated from the woman I love. Happiness had fired the first shots of a war that is being fought within me, but it immediately had to take cover.

"Lift your right foot, your left foot, alright bend over and spread 'em." No matter how many times I've heard those words and been coerced to perform these depreciating acts, each time, the embarrassment is renewed. Another man had commanded me to bend over to peer into my rectum. My eyes sing a song of hate as I glare at the correctional officer. Is that a spark of lust in his eyes? Rage and humiliation had happiness pinned down, firing salvo after salvo. With each round fired, I'm reminded of my powerlessness, but if I want to see my love this is what I must endure—the dressing room area of a penitentiary visiting room.

I changed into my visiting room attire, a flimsy brown jumpsuit, and I stepped into the visiting room. I glanced around, taking in my surroundings: hard plastic, brightly colored chairs are set up like a Greyhound bus station waiting area. Vending machines are lined up against the far wall with everything from bottled water to microwaveable chicken wings for sale. The paint on the walls was drab beige contributing to an atmosphere that's subdued. A low murmur of voices permeated the room; every once in a while, a snatch of a phrase, a word or two became distinguishable from the undertone. My head was on a swivel as I turned each time a word became distinctive. To my right a baby cried, to my left a couple argued, straight ahead a child screamed in delight. But then I looked towards the door where my wife would enter and all sounds became indistinguishable once more.

Then she entered and upon seeing me, she smiled, and her smile immediately joined the war waging within me, turning the tide. Humiliation was shot in the head and anger was on the run. My love walked into my open arms and, pressed her soft body against me. She squeezed me tight and just for an instant, I forgot where I was. All that existed was me and the warm embrace of the woman I love. We took a seat, lost in each other's presence, but only for a moment. For the joy that I felt came under assault anew by the oppressive weight the beast brings to bear. Cold, hard stares empty of compassion and electronic eyes watched our every move. The State was on high alert, for the expression of love through intimacy is a capital offense.

"Excuse me sir, could you please remove your hand." Anger stopped running, and I struggled to remain calm because if I didn't, there would be a heavy price to pay. So instead, I just removed my hand from my wife's knee and I glared at the correctional officer as he walked away. Despair replaced humiliation in the war. Anger had a new ally and together they launched an all-out offensive sending happiness ducking for cover. I wanted to touch her, kiss her, hold her tight and never let go, but like a storm cloud, a constant threat loomed over our heads. If I act on my natural desires, my visit will be terminated, my wife will be banned from the institution, and I will be placed in the restrictive housing unit, more infamously known as "the hole." So, although my wife was close, she felt miles away.

My physical contact has been reduced to minuscule spots of time and arbitrary enforcement of rules. These restrictions on physical interactions are constant erosions on a relationship that is swallowed whole by the insatiable hunger of a beast, causing me to feel utterly alone while in the midst of thousands. This artificial environment's very nature is designed to break all ties and reduce me to something other than what I was created to be. I've been left exposed, and in the process, an empty space has been revealed that's been filled with the tools of the beast: insecurities, paranoia, and jealousies. These tools work from within; they become a part of who I am, constructing in me a method of self-destruction that puts a chokehold on the relationship that I desperately fight to maintain.

Layer by layer, my humanity is being stripped away until I become a man devoid of the connections that make me whole. And now, after two decades of being confined, I've been completely contaminated. Paranoia, jealousy, and insecurities wreak havoc on my mind. I called my wife, and as the phone rang my heart raced—will this be the time that I call and she doesn't answer? When my wife tells me she's coming to see me, anxiously I wait for her, but will this be the time that she doesn't show? Every promise that I get from her is tainted by seeds of suspicion. Like a contagion, the infection of the beast spreads to my subconscious where it manifests in a dream that keeps repeating itself – why won't she answer the phone? Why can't I see her face?

Society has marked me, I've been designated a thing, incapable of redemption, unworthy of normal interactions. My wife's family and friends, influenced by these societal dictates, press her, they question her sanity, "Girl what's wrong with you? What can you get out of fucking with a jail bird? How can he provide for you, make love to you? Girl you crazy!"

Despite these circumstances, I've been able to capture this shadow, but the struggle to maintain it still remains. Although, I've been able to survive the ongoing battle with institutional obstacles, the self-sabotage and the pressure my wife faces from her family and friends, the beast's hunger is never sated. Until I'm completely devoured, it will continue to feed. But at the same time, I will continue to fight—I refuse to be eaten alive. God forbid that I succumb, that I stop fighting, for if I do, that hunger will have been satisfied – and I will have been totally consumed.

To love and be loved while doing time is an elusive thing and, as long as I'm trapped in the belly of the beast, I'll be forever chasing this shadow.

THE LETTER

Dear ?,

I find it quite difficult to write to someone I never met and explain – that I love you without knowing you – but I do. I find myself always thinking about what could have been had things not turned out the way they did. I can imagine your mother and how her stomach would be expanding as you developed in her womb. I can see in my mind my hands upon your mother's belly and how amazed I would be at feeling you kick. I can only imagine sitting in the doctor's office while he would allow me and your mother to listen to your rapidly beating heart and I would be humbled by the miracle of your existence. Oh, what I would give now to have been able to see your birth, to take your first breath, to cut your umbilical cord, to hear your first cry, and to be overwhelmed by that love that a father has for his child.

I picture myself and how I would be holding you in my arms, trying to comfort your cries. I can clearly see your tears sparkling like diamond chips as they form in the corner of your slanted eyes. I can hear your sobs that in my mind sound like the greatest love song ever written, and I can't help but to feel sad.

I can see you grow – transforming in front of my eyes – from a tiny helpless infant, to a curious toddler taking your first steps, to a young child with a thousand questions. When I picture your face, I can see myself, I can see your mother and I'm amazed that you can look like two different people at the same time.

Oh, how I regret not being able to raise you. How I can't share with you one of the most important lessons I learned in this life – how to love yourself – and how that lesson came at the expense of everything I held dear. It kills me that I can't look into your eyes and see the trust and the unconditional love trapped there and reflected back at me.

I wish I could share with you the story of why I came to be in this place and why things exist the way that they do. Finally, I just wish I had the chance to let you know that I'm sorry that I couldn't protect you when you needed my protection the most. I want to apologize for not being a better man for you and your mother. Because without my irresponsible behavior, you would have had the opportunity to live your life, instead of it ending before it even began.

Usually, when I was out doing my thing, I was always on point. I had to be if I wanted to survive. My line of work demanded it because the place where I plied my trade – the streets of West Philly – could be unforgiving to those who didn't pay attention, and on this night, I was one of those people.

I should've listened to my girl when she begged me to stay in the house. She came close to convincing me, too. I didn't notice when she got out of bed. I was busy on the phone, making arrangements for one of my spur-of-the-moment business meetings. It was only after I hung up the phone that I noticed she had left the room. While I was getting dressed she crept back into the bedroom. It was then that I noticed she was back. Not because she announced it, made a sound, or called out my name. It was almost as if she appeared out of thin air. The only reason why I knew she had returned was because I felt the silky smoothness of her nightgown and the softness of her body when she embraced me from behind.

"Baby, please don't go out there tonight. I just put the baby to sleep, and little Blue needs a little sister." Her voice, feathery soft, tickled my ear.

I spun in her arms. Gone was the scarf she had wrapped around her head. Instead, her hair hung loosely down her shoulders. The thick, cotton pajamas that she had on minutes before were replaced by a blood-red teddy. She blushed, displaying a deep set of dimples. Damn, she looked good. I stared into her dark brown eyes; they were pleading for me to stay. Then I felt her lips as soft kisses were placed on my face and neck. My baby was working that ole black magic. "Please, baby, don't go," she invoked softly into my ear.

I almost fell under her spell as thoughts of losing myself in her warm embrace danced in my mind. I shook it off. I had to get this money. I kissed her lightly on the forehead before reluctantly disengaging from her arms. She pouted, which made her look sexier. I shook my head. "Look, I'ma be right back. I got to go get this paper. I ain't gonna be gone long. Whatever you got in mind, keep it in mind 'cause I'ma be right back."

I could tell she still wanted to protest my leaving, but she relented, turned her back to me, and got into bed. Out of all the times I had to jump up in the middle of the night to handle some businesses, this was the first time she pleaded with me not to go. That should have been something I paid attention to. But, naw, not me I had to get that paper.

I was driven. At twenty-three years old, this was the only thing that I knew how to do. My father was a hustler. When I was a kid, my idols ain't dunk no fucking basketballs. My dad was who I wanted to be like. So, from the age of twelve, when that .40 caliber slug to the back of the head took him away from me, I'd been trying to fill his Ferragamos ever since. Once my dad was gone, my mother was devastated. His murder took a lot out of her, and to mask the pain of her loss she remarried. Her new husband, Mr. Crack Pipe, took everything she had left, effectively leaving me and my siblings to fend for ourselves. That left the weight of responsibility to fall squarely on my frail shoulders. At the tender age of twelve my childhood came to a screeching halt and I became the provider for me and my siblings. I gladly stepped my game up. After all, my father was my idol and I wanted nothing more than to be like him, so I stepped into my new role with the fervor of a zealot.

It wasn't a smooth ride. During that time, there were all kinds of setbacks, the worse happened at the age of eighteen. It cost me everything I had at the time plus four years of my life.

It ain't like God pressed the pause button on life while I did those four years. Life continued, and once I stepped out of those penitentiary gates the pressure was back on to get my paper up. At twenty-two I was still carrying my younger siblings, plus I had a family of my own that needed to eat, needed clothes, and needed a roof over their heads. On top of that it cost money to maintain my swag: the clothes, the jewels, the guns, the cars—that shit was expensive. I ain't gonna lie, it was a struggle. Fresh out the penitentiary, like most dudes, I ain't want to go back. I tried the job thing, but I was a convicted felon with no marketable skills. The jobs that were available to me left me with nothing after I paid the rent. It shouldn't be surprising that it took all of one year before I fell back on what I knew how to do best—hustle. But that didn't keep poverty from constantly nipping at my heels. I was always quick on my feet, so for the most part, I was able to stay one step ahead of being broke. I wasn't under any illusions. I knew from the murder of my father and the four years that I spent in prison that what I was doing could end in a flash with me losing my life or my freedom. So, I was gonna hustle and get as much as I could as fast as I could. Fuck the consequences. I would have rather been dead than either broke or in jail.

I took one more look at my girl. Her back was to me, and the covers were pulled up to her chin. She was pissed. I took a deep breath and exhaled. It was going to take some serious ass-kissing in order for me to make this right. I checked my Cartier watch; I had twenty-minutes to get to 52nd Street, where my transaction was taking place. Luckily, I only lived ten minutes away. Quickly I walked to my closet where I kept my safe. I opened it and pulled out a zip-lock bag with a half-a-kilo of some premium, high-grade cocaine. I also grabbed my .45-caliber handgun. Nothing made a business transaction go smoother than the threat of a hole tearing through flesh made from a .45-caliber slug. I put the cocaine in a brown paper bag, tucked my gun in the waistline of my sweatpants, and pulled the drawstrings tight. I then closed the door to my safe, grabbed my coat, put on my fitted Phillies baseball cap, pulled the brim low over my eyes, and headed towards my front door

It was a brisk, chilly, and rainy night when I stepped outside my apartment. It wasn't a steady type of rain, it was the kind of rain that floated—tiny droplets that seemed to be suspended in the night sky. Street lamps with their ominous glow lit up the sidewalk as I made my way to my car. Ten minutes later I was pulling up into the parking lot of a mini-market on 52nd and Spruce Street.

52nd Street, also known as the "Strip," was the main artery of West Philadelphia. It was a nine-block stretch of busy thoroughfares and businesses that provided everything the community needed. If you were hungry and had a taste for a home-cooked meal, soul food restaurants could be found by the aroma of the fried chicken and fish that filled the air. If you were on the move and needed a quick bite, the familiar arch of McDonalds was like a beacon that could be seen from blocks away. Greek-owned jewelry stores and clothing shops dotted the blocks along with Korean-owned convenience stores that sold everything from synthetic hair to potato chips. Up and down the blocks on both sides of the street, colorful beach umbrellas provided a little shade from the sun and protection from the rain for street vendors, their stands filled with everything from baseball caps to incense. Day and night shouts of "Hack man! Taxi hack!" rang loud as bootleg cabbies competed with Yellow Cab for their business. Twenty-four hours a day, seven days a week there was always something happening on the strip, which was perfect for me and my hustle.

I always conducted my business transactions on the Strip. It was kind of like hiding in plain sight. Only the extremely desperate stickup kids would risk a shoot-out in front of a lot of people. On top of all that, there were always police nearby. The Strip provided me with an unintended protection. But at the same time, I had to be on high alert, for the same thing that provided me this security could also lead to my loss of freedom.

I pulled up on the side of the mini-market and parked. My customer was already there. He stood only a few car lengths away, leaning on a dark blue Escalade. Now this particular customer of mine was not the stereotypical drug dealer. I mean he looked the part: fitted baseball cap, some

Timbs, a pair of jeans, a white tee, jewelry, and a black butter-leather jacket. What made him different? In my eyes, it was the mask. He didn't have one. This mask was a facial expression—stoic, eyes dead and intense. It was a face that read: *If you cross me I'll kill you.* Instead of this mask, this guy would always be smiling. He had a disposition that was so pleasant that it would immediately put you at ease, as if you had known him all your life. It wasn't just his temperament, but he would always want to talk. Not about business, women, sports, jewelry, or clothes, but he would want to talk about some deep philosophical shit. Like for example: a couple months prior to this particular day he asked me, "Ay, Blue, do you think the soul is separate from the body?"

"What?"

"I mean, you know how they say the body corrupts the soul? Do you believe that?"

"Listen, man, I ain't never thought about no shit like that. If it is, if it ain't, it doesn't matter to me. I'm trying to get this paper. If knowing that shit can get me a check, then school me about it. If not, I really don't give a fuck."

"Yeah, you right. I just be thinking about stuff like that from time to time."

"Yeah, well, maybe you in the wrong line of work."

There was another time that sticks out in my mind. Around the same time, and once again right after we finished our transaction. I shook his hand and was trying to get away from him before he asked me one of his weird questions. I couldn't get away fast enough. Right as I turned to walk to my car, he stopped me, "Yo, Blue." With his usual smile he asked me, "Yo, Blue, do you think what we're doing is evil?"

I looked at this crazy motherfucker and said, "I'm taking care of my family, and if that's evil, well I guess I'm an evil motherfucker."

He tilted his head, looked at me, his smile never fading. "If selling poison to people ain't evil, then what is?"

I was a little puzzled by this question. I found myself thinking, *Is this motherfucker the police?* Naw, I doubt it. I had been dealing with him for some time. If he was the police, I would've been arrested a long time ago. I shook that thought off and answered him. "Evil is not doing whatever you can to make sure your family has something to eat, somewhere to sleep, something to wear."

"Yeah, but what if in doing that, you take away someone else's ability to do the same for their family?"

He would always ask me questions like that, so as I approached him I steeled my resolved—I was not going to indulge him in one of his weird conversations. After all, I had to get back to my woman and the promise she had in her eyes.

I was so preoccupied in my own thoughts that I wasn't paying attention. So, when I looked up, I was staring down the barrel of a gun, and this guy had the nerve to be smiling. It wasn't a fake smile where the smile doesn't match the eyes, it was genuine. It was his smile, that smile that seemed so out of place for the kind of life we were living. It was so disarming that I began to think he was playing. But he couldn't be. I didn't know him well enough for him to put a gun in my face and it be a game. As these thoughts were tip-toeing through my mind, something changed. His smile evaporated, replaced by a look of sadness that was so intense I forgot that he held a gun, and I almost asked him what was wrong. Before I could figure out all this strange behavior, the muzzle of his gun flashed, gunpowder exploded and everything went black.

I awoke to the sound of someone calling my name. "Blue, wake up, Blue."

My eyes fluttered and cracked open to the brilliant rays of the sun. I shut them. I was confused. Where was I? I slowly cracked my eyes open to allow them time to adjust to the brightness. I slowly began to take in my surroundings. I was lying in a field of grass. That's when I noticed the morning dew soaking through my clothes. One by one my senses began to come back on line. My ears were filled with the sounds of nature; I could hear water flowing from a nearby stream and the sounds of insects clicking and birds whistling. I sat up, my bewilderment growing, and then my memory returned. A rainy night in the mini-market parking lot, my customer, a gun, his smile, sadness, and a gunshot. My heart began to pound. Frantically, I began checking myself for gunshot wounds. There weren't any. *What the fuck is going on? Am I crazy?*

"Blue."

That voice. Not only could I hear it, but in a weird way I could feel it as well. It was like I took a sip of a nice hot cup of tea. This voice filled me with warmth. I turned around and there he was, his smile erasing all my confusion away and filling me with anger. It was my customer. I couldn't stop from exploding with fury. "Motherfucker, you shot me!"

"Did I?"

"Yeah, motherfucker!"

"Where are you shot at?"

I checked my body again, knowing full well I would not find any gunshot wounds. "Yo, man, what the fuck is going on? I remember you shot me. We were on the Strip. You were meeting me to cop a half-a-brick. Yo, man, where the fuck am I? How did I get here?"

"What you remember, Blue, is an image your mind produced to explain what happened to you."

Butterflies, the size of hawks took flight in the pit of my gut, my heart began to pound. "What you mean? What happened to me?"

You were in your car driving to meet me when you were sideswiped by a semi. You never saw it coming. Everything you remember about meeting me was a fiction created by your mind in that split second between the impact of the crash, the loss of consciousness and death."

Dead? How could that be? I was still alive. I began to feel my face. I could hear, I could see, how could I be dead? What the fuck did he mean dead? I looked around and took notice of my surroundings: the green of the grass, the trees full of foliage. I noticed the air for the first time. It was clean, fresh, pure. I was in an unfamiliar place. I wasn't supposed to be here. What happened to the Strip? Where was I? What was this place? I couldn't hear the sound of tires rolling over the asphalt, or loud music. Where were all the people? I couldn't smell exhaust from cars or that fried chicken and fish aroma that filled the air up down 52nd

Street. Where were the familiar voices of old-time hustlers calling out, "Hack man, Taxi hack!" I looked around at the natural beauty that surrounded me and realization began to dawn. Small pools of tears formed in the corner of my eyes before cascading down my cheeks. I was dead.

Automatically, I began to think of my woman. my one-year-old son, my mother, my siblings, and the rest of my loved ones. Like the devastating power of a tsunami, grief flooded my being in wave after wave. At that point, my death became secondary as the realization that I had been snatched away from everyone that I loved settled over me.

"Blue, you'll see them again."

"Wait a minute. How did you know what I was thinking? Who the fuck is you? Why are you here? I shook my head. *This can't be real. I was dreaming. Yeah, that's it, this is a dream. Wake up, Blue.* I squeezed my eyes shut and shook my head again. I began to count. "1-2-3-4-5-6-7-8-9-10." I opened my eyes, expecting to be home. I wasn't. I was still in that field of grass.

"Blue, this isn't a dream."

Resignation began to settle over me. I began to think about how I lived my life. All the terrible acts I committed began to dance in my mind's eye. My heart began to pound again as fear chased my grief away. Now what? I knew I would have to pay. I looked at my customer again. Was he God?

He smiled, "I'm what you would think of as an angel. The Creator is vast, so omniscient, it would be impossible for your mind to process his being.

"You know what's impossible for me to process? A crack-selling angel. Come on, man, an angel? You were selling coke."

"Did you ever witness me selling cocaine?"

"Naw, but you were copping from me. What, you were getting high? Shit, that's worse, a crackhead angel. What, you got kicked out of heaven because you couldn't stop getting high? Come on with this shit. Where am I?"

He chuckled, "Blue, I told you, you're dead. And this place is a temporary one. A place that only serves to get you ready. As far as me buying cocaine from you. I had to establish a relationship with you. In order for me to accomplish that I had to become a part of your world. How else could I establish a relationship with you? If I would have revealed to you that I was an angel, not only would it have taken a tremendous effort to convince you of that truth, but once I was able to convince you it would have changed the trajectory of your life. I had to allow you to live your life without interference and at the same time establish a relationship with you."

"A relationship for what? Then you gonna say that you're a guardian angel and in the same breath say that you weren't trying to get me to change my life, even though I was living foul. I'm not getting this. If not to prevent me from doing nut shit, why even bother?"

"Because, Blue, I needed to be familiar with you."

"For what?"

"So that when you arrived here you could have someone familiar to explain things. It makes it a whole lot easier for people to accept the seemingly impossible if it's coming from someone they're familiar with."

I shook my head again. I knew what I was in store for. "Well, I know I was about that life and it deserves only one particular kind of punishment. But in my defense. I only played the hand I was given. Jesus Christ being my lord and savior wasn't putting food on the table, crack was. And at the end of the day, if I had to be under the same circumstances, I'd still be a crack-selling motherfucker. Oh, wait a minute, is cussing a sin too? As a matter of fact, just tell me how hot the fire is."

My customer chuckled again. "What do you think hell is?"

"What you mean? Hell is where you go when you live a life doing all kinds of foul shit. It's a place where you burn forever."

"What if I told you that's not true? Let me ask you this. Do you love your son?"

I almost asked him how he knew that I had a son, but, then remembered he could read my mind. Why wouldn't he know that I had a son? So instead I just answered him. "Of course, I love my son."

"Alright, think of the worst thing that he could do. Would the punishment for whatever he did last forever?"

"No. I would punish him, but I would make sure he understood what he did, and that it was wrong, why it was wrong, why he was being punished, and I'd make sure that he learned from it."

Okay, what if he already knew what he did was wrong? Would that justify punishing him forever?"

"What? What kind of question is that? I love my son. I ain't got it in me to see him suffer at all let alone forever."

"Blue, do you believe God loves you?"

"Man, I don't know. I never even thought about it."

"Well I can assure you, he does. So, with that being the case, why would God treat his children any differently than you would treat yours?"

"You are acting like I made this shit up. I'm only telling you what these religions be saying. The Bible and the Quran talk about heaven and hell. If you're good you go to heaven, if you're bad you go to hell. Heaven is for the true believers, and I ain't believed in shit except getting that paper. I was a foul dude. So, I already know those rivers of milk and honey ain't for me."

"Blue, you remember when I asked you about good and evil?"

"Yeah. At the time, I just thought you was on some weirdo shit. But, yeah, I remember."

"Blue, people aren't inherently evil. God, in his infinite wisdom, created human beings with imperfections. Because of these inherent weaknesses, people are susceptible to the influences that exists in their environments. But, you see, this in itself is perfection."

"What?"

"Think about it like this, if you were perfect there would be no need to strive for anything. But you have faults, weaknesses; these shortcomings manifest in different ways and they affect every aspect of your life. Because of this, life is full of trials that push you to your limits. In doing so, either you're able to overcome your shortcomings, you figure out what they are, and work on eliminating them or you succumb to them and become a slave to circumstance. Blue, weakness was necessary to provide human beings with the motivation to want more. This was why I said the perfection was in the imperfection.

"Also, human beings don't live in vacuums. They exist in environments that have all kinds of influences, some positive some negative. Whatever your shortcomings are, they will determine how these influences affect you. In essence, your faults and your ability to overcome them and the process in which all this takes place is what gives purpose to life. It makes life worth living. So, Blue, it's not that people are evil, it's just that people succumb to their weaknesses, and as a result commit evil acts."

"I hear you, and it makes sense, but what part does the devil play in all that?"

"Blue, do you think for one minute that God created the devil without knowing his nature? The way the story goes about the devil is told, it gives the impression that the devil rebelled against the will of God and it was unexpected. The devil was created for a purpose. This purpose was to do exactly what he did and has been doing. Remember, human beings are not perfect; they have weaknesses, so in comes the devil to tempt human beings. He pushes them, goads them into giving in to their weaknesses. But, Blue, this is all a part of God's creation. So why would God allow you to burn forever for being what he created you to be?"

"Yo, man, I'm confused. Why would God allow people to spread false information? So many people believe the wrong things."

"But, Blue, don't you see? There is no right and wrong thing to believe. What you see from humans are intelligent beings trying to make sense of their world and to create societies with as little chaos as possible. You see, Blue, at the end of the day when people die, just like you, they'll be in a place similar to this place, and that's when their true education will begin. Once they're educated properly, they will then make their transition."

"Transition to what?"

"We haven't gotten to that point yet. Before we do, there is something fundamental that you have to understand. Blue, every living thing is connected. We all are connected through the breath of God that gives us life. When people become disconnected from the knowledge that everything alive is a child of God, in comes the suffering that humans endure. Why do you think people can kill one another in the name of God? That's almost like you killing your son in the name of your father. People do this because they're oblivious to this connection. Their relationship with God becomes individualized. They become God's chosen people and all other people become the infidels, the kaffirs, the non-believers, the heretics. If people don't adhere to the various religious dogmas, they cease to be the children of God or even human. They become the harbingers of sin, not deserving to live. The earth and all other living things become objects, a means to an end that exists only to satisfy individual wants and needs. Because of this, not only do human beings directly destroy themselves, but they destroy the environment as well. You see, it's easy to abuse the earth if you don't recognize your connection to it. But, if you are aware of this fundamental information, you become insulated from the negative influences that affect so many others."

Silenced engulfed us both as I contemplated everything I was just told. Everything that I had ever learned was flipped on its head. *What the fuck he mean there ain't no devil? No hell?* A jumble of feelings was flowing through my mind; extreme sadness. I was dead and although I also learned that I would see my loved ones again it was something about not being able to go home that killed me inside. Confusion, nothing I had grown up to believe was the truth. I mean, I believed In God. I went to church when I was little. When I spent those four years in prison, I tried the Muslim thing. But, life and just trying to survive left me no time for religion. God, what happens after you die, good and evil, were things I never thought about. I was a marginal believer at best. What about all those people who were fanatical about their beliefs? I shook my head. I began to think about this connection my customer was talking about. My mind rebelled. *How was I related to grass, to trees?*

"Blue, you're thinking about it in the wrong way. Look at it like this; all forms of life on earth support one another to live. You want to know how you're related to grass, to trees. Well, the grass and the trees need carbon dioxide to live. They take in the carbon and simultaneously give off oxygen this is a part of a process called photosynthesis. Human beings and the other animals breathe in oxygen and breathe out carbon dioxide. Without one the other couldn't exist. This is your connection to the grass and trees. All life on earth is connected directly or indirectly creating a perfect balance. But, because most human beings are unaware of this connection they over indulge. Like I mentioned earlier they pollute the air and the seas. They overfish the oceans and kill off whole species of animals. They're destroying this balance, threatening all life as you know it."

My customer's words dissipated the fog of lack of apprehension. Now I understood. I could see this connection. I closed my eyes and ran my fingers through the grass. I noticed for the first time the texture. It was smooth on one side and slightly abrasive on the other. It felt alive. I opened my eyes and the miracle of life and this connection became tangible. My imagination exploded in my mind. I could see the process of photosynthesis taking place, and I was in awe. I smiled.

My customer nodded his head. "Now you see."

I nodded my head in response.

"Blue, now that you have this new appreciation for life; it's time for you to make your transition. You'll be going to a place where you'll live again. But this time you'll be able to live life with the knowledge of this connection, surrounded by people with the same understanding. Everyone who ever passed away before you will be there, living in harmony with everything around them. You'll be reunited with all your loved ones who have passed on, and one day everyone who you left behind will be joining you there. You won't have to wait long for them either. Every two days that passes by where you're going, equals a year back on earth. So, before you know it, your family will be joining you. But, Blue, I must warn you, if for any reason, you do something contrary to what being connected to all living things is, you'll cease to exist in that place. You'll be removed and sent back to earth to be born again, minus the knowledge of your previous existence. You'll be born, you'll die, you'll make another transition, and if you transgress again the process will begin anew. Do you understand?"

"Yeah. But, what if I decide to transgress just so I can be born again?"

"Blue, once you become a conscious being, the punishment for transgressing will be severe. Not only will you be born again and live a life as a new person, but right before death claims you again, the loss of all that you love in that life and your previous one will be felt. To lose the people you love over and over again is far worse than any hellfire. You see, the objective is to get you to understand what it means to love yourself and everything connected to you, because in doing that you'll automatically love God because the Creator is the thread that connects us all."

I nodded my head in understanding. I was confident. I knew that I would never cross that line? But I was a little curious, "How often do people transgress?"

"More than you would think?"

"Why do you think that is?"

"Besides the fact that it's a part of God's plan, I can only guess. But in my humble opinion, it just takes some people more time than others to get the full meaning of things."

"So, what's next for me?"

"Well, if you're ready, you can continue your journey. Are you ready?"

I took a deep breath and slowly exhaled. "Yeah, man, I think I'm ready."

"Okay, close your eyes, Blue…"

"Wait! Will I see you again?"

My customer smiled. That same smile that in another life seemed so out of place but now seemed so appropriate. "No, Blue. I was created to prepare people for their transition, and there are countless others I have to attend. Now, are you ready?"

I nodded my head and closed my eyes.

"Blue, keep your eyes closed until you hear voices. Blue, what I just said is vital. Whatever you do, don't open your eyes until that point."

I nodded my head once again before all went silent. For a few seconds, I felt nothing. Butterflies began to stir in the pit of my gut as anticipation began to build. Suddenly, I felt a jolt, causing the butterflies to explode into flight. I squeezed my eyes tighter as I began to feel lighter. It was almost like my body was losing its substance. The feeling intensified until it felt like the only thing left of me was my consciousness floating in space. I could feel nothing, hear nothing, and although my eyes were closed, I got this sensation that I was drifting in absolute blackness. Out of nowhere I was falling, faster, faster. I began to panic. I almost opened my eyes, but I remembered my customer's instructions: "Blue, whatever you do, keep your eyes closed." I resisted the urge. I fought the panic. The feeling intensified. Suddenly as quick as it began it was over and all was still.

I could feel again. No more weird sensations of nothingness, floating, or falling. I could feel a warm breeze as it gently caressed my skin. I could hear running water in the distance, the birds' chirping their melodic songs of life, the sound of leaves rustling in the trees, and then a man's voice.

"Blue."

There was something familiar about that voice. Slowly I opened my eyes. My breath caught as my heart began to pound. I was staring into a pair of eyes that were identical to my own. Eyes that belonged to a man who passed away more than ten years ago. Eyes that I thought I would never be able to gaze into again.

The man smiled. "Welcome home, son."

Early in my life—before I had facial hair and my life was not complicated by overdue bills, the care of children and trying to figure out my purpose in life—every once in a while, I would notice these two strangers. They seemed to be good friends and more often than not, they would be together. The first of the two went by the name of *Time*. He was a young man with a body like one of those guys you see on billboards modeling Calvin Klein underwear. Whenever I saw him he would be wearing the same outfit; white tee shirt, blue jeans, and some Timberland boots with metal taps on the soles. He was a handsome young man with black, curly hair, caramel complexion, piercing brown eyes that sparkled with mischief and a smile that was so infectious. No matter how bad my day was going, that smile would make it all better. He was full of vigor and always energetic—which caused him to move at a breakneck pace as if he was always running late.

His partner went by the name of *Death*. He was a little bit older and a little overweight. He always wore white outfits: white hat, white tennis shoes and white pants that were always baggy as if he was ashamed of his size. He had these lifeless, hazel, hooded eyes that were matched by a face crisscrossed by old battle scars. He never smiled. Instead, he would always be smirking. Whenever I heard the adults speak of him, the occasions were always sad and tinted with fear—a fear that I unknowingly inherited and that would manifest itself in my dreams. I would be running, with Death close on my heels. I'd hear his grunts as his feet pounded on the ground behind me. Out of nowhere I would always trip and stumble to the ground.

Death would loom over me, he'd reach for me, with these long, dirty, razor sharp, claw-like finger nails. Right before he would grab me, I would wake up, heart pounding drenched in sweat. Just as quickly as that dream would end, I'd forget about Death until the next time.

Death was different from Time in the sense that Time never invaded my dreams and Death moved at an entirely different pace. Death was more deliberate and slower, almost calculated as if he measured every step he took. They were the exact opposite of one another, but at the same time perfect for each other. This was evident whenever I noticed them together. During these moments, it seemed as if they were engaged in this game with the adults in the neighborhood. Time, the young and fitter of the two, would always be chasing them, while Death hid, waiting in ambush. It was like this weird game of Tag, one that they could never lose—although they would both always be "it", and whomever was unlucky enough to be caught was never seen or heard from again.

Neither of them had any relevance to me personally; other than seeing Time and Death chase after the adults, they existed only in the periphery of my life. But every once in a while, they both would slip out of the margins and make themselves known to me personally. On occasions when Time made his presence known, it seemed as if my days would pass by a lot quicker.

For instance, when I was a boy—after school was out and my homework was done—I would be outside riding my bike, chasing girls, playing tops, or catching bugs. You know, just having fun like young boys do. Suddenly, I would see Time. He would speed by with these long quick strides. Before

I knew it, the sun would be descending behind neighborhood row homes, street lights would be lighting up and mom would be calling me home.

Time's quick strides would be a blur in the corner of my eye in the summertime and before the sound of his metal-tipped boots clicking on the concrete would fade from my ears, the shouts and laughter of children playing in the summertime heat was replaced by school bells ringing in the fall.

The funny thing about these sightings were sometimes it seemed as if he would catch me watching him and he would change his appearance. Like, I'd be in school, sitting in class bored and anxious for school to be over. I'd take a quick glance out of the classroom window and see Time power-walking through the playground. On occasions like these, he would notice me watching him. He would pause, nod his head, smile and right before my eyes magically transform. He would go from a young man to a feeble, gray-haired old man, bent at the waist, with a walking stick in his hand. His new white tee shirts would transform to an old one with the material so worn out I would be able to see through it. His blue jeans would be faded and frayed to the point where I could see the flaking of his skin peeking through the holes that exposed his knees. He would hold my gaze for a moment while still smiling then wink, right before turning and continuing to shuffle along in slow motion, scraping his metal tipped Timbs across the asphalt of the playground. At those times, it seemed as if my school day, which only lasted for a few hours, took days to end.

When I got older, I would still see Time. I'd be in the club holding my girl close, our bodies moving in time with R.

Kelly's smooth voice singing about some *Honey Love*. Strobe lights would flash in the darkness and out of nowhere Time would glide by on the crowded dance floor, dancing too fast to love songs. Before I could even laugh at the ridiculousness of his non-rhythmic dancing, the lights in the club would flicker off and on, signaling *last call for alcohol*.

This was also the period in time when Death would escape the margins of my life. On rare occasions, I would notice him with his dead eyes, scarred face and perpetual smirk. But now that I think back on it, it would be on the same occasions when he would pop up in my dreams. Every time, it would be right after that weird game of tag was ending with Time skipping away as some unlucky soul found themselves trapped by Death. Whoever it was would just be gone, never to be seen or heard from again. At this point, no one close to me had ever gotten trapped in this weird game of tag. So, although I would notice that some of the adults in the neighborhood would be missing and others would just be sad, for me, when someone fell into Time and Death's ambush, it was just something I noticed. There was no emotional investment; it was just some distant occurrence that had no bearing on my life.

****

On June 6, 1992, my relationship with Time and Death changed. It was one of those events in life while you're in the moment that it's happening, you're oblivious to its impact, and you only realize the significance of it years later. For me it was no different as Time and Death ensnared me in their deadly game.

It was one of those record-breaking summer evenings. The air was thick with moisture and as still as a statue. The heat was stifling, oppressive and it clung to me like the embrace of a desperate lover. I was in my early twenties, on the cusp of manhood, lost, a stranger to myself and addicted to anything that felt good. On this particular night I was in heaven, enjoying the effects of the heat on the codeine that polluted my bloodstream. As I nodded in and out of awareness I was oblivious as Time funneled me into Death's ambush. When Death sprung his trap, I was caught off guard. There was no pain at least not in the physical I-just-got-shot kind of way. It was more like a how-stupid-can-you-be type of shock; after all I was in the ninth month of being on the run for a homicide, and with all the brilliance of a twenty-three-year-old, I figured the best place to hide was the first place the police would look for me—my neighborhood. It was sort of a stupid version of hiding in plain sight. But now that I think back on it, it was a stupor, a side effect of the codeine coursing through my bloodstream and I was just high rather than in shock.

Cold metal handcuffs bit into my wrists and for a moment I climbed out of my stupor. In that moment of clarity, I felt Death's cold hands began to squeeze.

"You fuckin murderer! We finally got your black ass! You'll never see the outside of a prison wall again." Harsh words shot from the detective's mouth. They cut through the hot, humid air. My body jerked as if his words were bullets that penetrated my flesh. I stumbled. Rough hands gripped tight, steadying me, not to protect me from injury, but to prevent any slick escape attempt—and also to be used as an excuse to inflict some pain. The detective yanked my cuffed hands that were behind my back and lifted them upwards. I was forced to bend over awkwardly at the waist as daggers of pain shot through my shoulders. Suddenly, I was weightless. My feet dangled in midair before he tossed me face first into a black maw. As I rode air currents of pain on Fear's back, out of the corner of my eye I caught a glance of Time as that feeble old man and he was shaking Death's hand. I began to panic. My life flashed through my mind right before I landed in the back of a police van. Pain exploded throughout my body and purple light flashed in my eyes. My head spun as I tried to get my bearings. A loud bang. The police van doors slammed shut and I was swallowed alive in Death's trap.

When the effects of the codeine wore off, I found myself in the county jail. At 140 pounds, I was lost in a bright orange jumpsuit and oblivious to the seriousness of my situation. Instead of preparing myself for what lay ahead, my days were spent gambling Little Debbie snack cakes and cigarettes. Time was there also. I only saw him once and it was a quick glance. I almost didn't recognize him with his tight-ass jumpsuit as he moved at that breakneck pace, but then he paused for just a second and smiled. Before I knew it six months had streaked by and I found myself sitting in a courtroom.

Bang, Bang, Bang! "Order in the court!" The pounding of the wooden gavel and the judge's shout exploded like gunshots in the confines of the crowded courtroom, killing the murmur of the crowd. The judge cleared his throat and glared at me. "Will the defendant please stand." He pronounced each of his next words slowly and deliberately, as if they would be the last words I would ever hear. Malice dripped from his voice, "I find you guilty of murder in the second degree which carries a mandatory sentence of life without the possibility of parole."

I sat in that courtroom and found myself head bowed, staring at the lines of the tilted floor. Although I heard the judge's words and I understood what those words of condemnation meant, I refused to believe them. *Forever* was a concept that my young mind lacked the capacity to process. I refused to believe in the possibility that my life could be one where I spent decades living in prison only to die there. That was not how I envisioned my life would be.

I slowly raised my head and took stock of all the pain that echoed through the sobs of my loved ones and the hurt that was apparent in the tears staining their faces. I locked eyes with Time. He had transformed once again and this time he closely resembled his partner Death. He was dressed in an all-white suit and those piercing brown eyes were devoid of that spark of mischief. They were lifeless, hooded. His infectious smile was also gone. Normally relaxed, his body was tense as if he was poised to strike. But he didn't strike; instead he smirked as if the loss of my freedom was something to be mocked. I glared angrily at him, long and hard. I shouted threats at him and lunged angrily at him. But Time didn't budge. He didn't respond at all to my idle threats. In that fast power-like stride, he just turned his back to me and simply walked away. By then, Time was no longer a stranger. He had become my bitter enemy.

As I left that courtroom handcuffed and shackled on my way to board a Blue Goose prison bus, all I could think of was Time and how much I hated him: *I find you guilty of murder in the second degree, which carries a sentence of life without the possibility of parole.* This feeling was my constant companion. It stayed with me as I traveled from the county jail to a state penitentiary.

When I found myself residing in a state penitentiary trapped behind forty-foot walls topped with razor wire, motion detectors and interspersed with towers manned by guards armed with assault rifles, I was in a daze. Separated from everything and everyone I loved, I retreated into a prison of my own construction and it would be years before I figured out what it meant to truly be free.

As I fortified the walls of my inner prison, my hatred for Time ran out of fuel—I simple became indifferent towards him. This indifference created a duality, where sometimes he was like distant relative, a cousin ten times removed, that lives down South that I never saw—he's related to me, but there was no relationship. On other occasions, he was like a close family member who'd always be there. Because of this, I would take him—like I did them—for granted. That's the best way that I can describe how our relationship was by then.

Although I had become indifferent towards Time, it seemed like to Time, I had become an object of obsession. No one was deserving of my thoughts, love, or attention except him. Like a jealous friend, Time began to subtly come between as many of my relationships as he could. With a well-placed whisper, *Terrell ain't never getting out of prison. You might as well get on with your life.* Before I knew it, people that I once knew and loved became strangers to me as they began to listen to those whispers and drop out of my life. No matter what I did to reconnect those severed bonds, Time would kick up some dust, and year after year when the dust had settled, I was left alone holding the tattered remains of those broken ties.

During the first eight years of my incarceration, as Time sabotaged my relationships, he no longer shuffled by slowly as a feeble old man. The minute I stepped inside those forty-foot walls, Time appeared to me as that young man. But instead of simply walking at a quick pace, he moved with a record–breaking speed of a world-class sprinter. Every tenth of a second the clicking of his metal-tipped boots echoing in the hallways of the prison marked his passage and before I knew it I had aged eight years, although it felt like I had just arrived. You see, my mind was in rebellion against reality. I'd been condemned to die in prison and the best way that I knew how to cope was to act as if my condemnation wasn't real. So, I focused on the immediate. I immersed myself in the daily prison existence: I played cards, chess, sports, I read books, I exercised, listened to stories, and I told stories about the women I had mistreated in the past, the drugs I had sold, the robberies I had committed, the jewelry and the clothes I had worn and the cars I used to drive; while my nights were filled with dreams of getting back to a life I no longer had. Life in the penitentiary was fast paced and my days passed by in a blur. It was just like it was when I was younger when Time would step out of the periphery of my life and I would see him in the club gliding by as he danced too fast to love songs. The minute I saw Time sprinting through those dim corridors, those first eight years of my incarceration went by just as fast. Only now there were no clubs, no dancing too fast to love songs and Death was conspicuously absent.

****

By the turn of the new millennium I noticed that instead of seeing Time every once in a blue I would see him every day. I noticed that Time no longer moved like a world-class sprinter, for he had transformed into that feeble old man. Simultaneously life in the penitentiary had slowed to a crawl. It no longer felt like I had just arrived, but instead it felt like I had been in prison forever. For eight years, Time had been sprinting at that record-breaking pace and only when I accepted the truth about my circumstance did he seem to slow down. It had taken me eight years, but I finally came to the realization that it was a strong possibility that I would grow old and die behind those forty-foot walls. By immersing myself in the daily routine of prison life I neglected to do anything that could have changed that possibility.

During that same period, his partner, Death had reappeared; he and Time resumed their game. From the year 2000 to 2015, every so often someone I loved would get caught in their trap: my father, my step-father, my grandmother, my grandfather, my brother, my little sister, my cousin, my uncle and one of my childhood friends. But Time and Death's game of Tag wasn't an exclusive thing that was only reserved for those outside of those forty-foot walls. It was the kind of game that transcended boundaries. All around me I began to notice that the men I had been around for years were being funneled by Time into Death's snare as well.

With each episode of loss, I'd find myself back in that courtroom face to face with Time. He would be dressed in an all-white suit; his eyes would be dead and hooded and that mocking smirk would be plastered across his face. This vision would be a painful reminder of what my life had become: an endless parade of occasions where I'd be trapped in a world of hopelessness and despair with no means of escape.

There was no refuge in my dreams, for my dreams had become a place haunted by the faces of loved ones who were no longer there and tainted by the despair that dogged my every waking hour. Every time I drifted off to sleep I'd find myself walking down a familiar street, shaking hands, laughing and talking with my homies from the old neighborhood. But before I could get to where I was going, the row homes of the neighborhood would be gone and I would find myself on a prison cell block. Instead of shaking hands, laughing and talking with old friends I would be alone walking through a gauntlet of stone-faced prison guards, dressed in black, their knuckles white as they gripped four-foot long night sticks. My heart would be pounding as I anticipated blows that would never come. Other times I would be stepping out of my home but instead of being greeted by the shouts of laughter and joy of children playing on a city block, I would be greeted by a dusty prison yard surrounded by a forty-foot wall, filled with men in brown prison uniforms walking aimlessly around a dirt track. My dreams were no longer just dreams because they would always morph into these nightmares, killing one of my last means of escape.

Through all the pain and longing to be free I would still see Time with his tattered, worn clothes hanging off his weak and frail shoulders. He would be shuffling up and down the penitentiary's dim corridors with the familiar sound of his metal-tipped boots scraping against the waxed floors. For some strange reason, he would always be singing, with a voice as soothing as a summer breeze. His song would provide me with a little comfort:

I was born by the river
In a little tent
Whooaa just like a river
I've been running ever since
It's been a long, long time coming
But I know change gone come...

And yet, even with the comfort his voice provided me, I would always find myself thinking, *Why the fuck is he always singing this old ass song?*

****

On June 6, 2015, I had reached a milestone—my twenty-third year residing in a state penitentiary. On the morning of that day I stepped into the prison yard into the brilliant rays of the sun and there was Time staring me in the eyes. For the past fifteen years, he had been singing that old song. But on this day, there was no singing, he just stared at me with this knowing smile. Because it was on that day at the age of forty-six that I realized I had lived twenty-three years outside of a prison wall and twenty-three years within the confines of a prison wall.

Those first twenty-three years had produced a man that no mother would be proud of. I was walled in behind facades of what I thought would protect me, of what I believed people would accept me as. I had developed a false sense of consciousness that resulted in a perverted world view that took me down a path that led to half of my life languishing in a maximum-security prison. It was on June 6, 2015 when I stepped into that prison yard that it dawned on me, when I was arrested way back in "92", who I was for those first twenty-three years of my life had been chased by Time into Death's waiting arms. For the first eight years of my incarceration I struggled to stay alive. I retreated further behind the facades that had been protecting me for most of my life. My false consciousness became my life support system that allowed me to desperately cling to the life I had known. But Death removed the bricks of those facades of self-protection and others' expectations right before his claw-like hands grabbed the cord of my false consciousness and yanked out the plug of my life support. The walls to my inner prison came tumbling down and who I used to be flat lined. As Time shuffled along singing that old Sam Cooke song, it was on June 6, 2015 that I finally understood why—he was singing my requiem.

But that wasn't the end of me. For Death's trap had become a womb of consciousness and I was reborn. Once I emerged, I finally realized what it meant to truly be free. My past mistreatment of women, the drugs, the robberies, the clothes, jewelry and the cars were not stories told to fill monotonous days, they were the very things that imprisoned me. So, when Death removed the bricks of my inner prison and yanked out the plug of my life support, that realization provided me the freedom to move beyond the things that placed limitation on what I could be.

Old man Time, weak, bent at the waist, walking stick in hand, has been inching along. As he slowed, the beating of my heart matches the scraping of his metal-tipped boots. My heart pounds to keep pace as Time once again funnels me towards Death's ambush. I understand that on this go around when I'm caught, it won't be symbolic. I can see Death hiding, waiting in ambush, and I know he's waiting for me. I'm okay with this inevitability because I understand that Time funnels everyone into Death's trap and once Death's clawed hands gets a hold of you, there is no escape. Even his partner Time dies—betrayed by Death. But as soon as that second-hand clicks past the twelve, Time is reborn into a new day.

Death no longer invades my dreams and the fear that was passed on to me when I was a child is no more. Now I understand that although Death looks frightening with his battle-scarred face and his perpetual sneering, he's necessary. Because without Death lying in ambush, how could I truly appreciate life?

Right now, Time is no longer a stranger. I no longer hate him, nor am I indifferent towards him. That duality does not exist. Time is no longer like that cousin ten times removed or that close family member that I had taken for granted. I've become a man who's finally realized how important Time is. Each scrape of his metal-tipped boots is as precious as each beat of my heart. No one has been a part of my life as long as or as much as he has. Whether as that young man moving at that breakneck pace or as that old man shuffling along in slow motion I finally learned not to take his presence for granted. At this point in my life everything I do, every decision I make, is made with Time in mind. My whole life revolves around him, and because of this, I now understand how big of a part he has played in my life. Without Time chasing me into Death's trap, I would have never experienced a rebirth in my own life. I'd still be walled in behind facades of self-protection and other expectations. I would have lived the rest of my life under a false consciousness and as a stranger to myself. My potential to be more would have remained locked away within my inner prison, never being able to realize what it means to truly be free and a life lived like that, is a life not worth living at all.

The flickering, pale glow of a black-and-white floor-model television illuminated the front room of my grandmother's home. The light reflected off the pictures of her twelve children that were lovingly hung on the wall opposite the television, giving them an almost angelic glow. I can recall staring at those photographs and smiling with delight when I recognized the younger versions of my aunts and uncles. Worn-down carpet covered the hardwood floor, and it would make my legs itch as I tried to get comfortable leaning against the soft flesh of my grandmother's legs. She would be sitting in her favorite chair that, after years of usage, was molded perfectly to fit the contours of her body. The odor of Ben Gay that my grandmother used for her aching back would fill my nostrils. Oh, how I hated that old rug and the odor of my grandmother's muscle rub. But her voice, melodic in its inflection like the griots of old, recounted ancient tales. Images of a serpent whispering in Eve's ear, Moses splitting the Red Sea, Jonah being swallowed by a whale, the powerful Samson bringing down the columns of a Philistine's home, and Lot's wife turning into a pillar of salt, would all play in my mind like an epic motion picture. My eyes would be closed and my grandmother's voice would be the vehicle that took me to a place where miracles were a reality and Jehovah walked the earth interacting with His creation. I was a five-year-old sitting in that cozy front room, and although I hated that old rug and the smell of her muscle rub, her voice recounting those tales was worth the slight discomfort.

I loved those Old Testament stories and the time I spent sitting at my grandmother's knee. It was my own little world, landlocked by borders of my limited imagination where God walked the earth with men and miracles were possible. But it was also a time when doubt first made its presence known. A slight nudge in the back and I stumbled across the boundaries that those Old Testament stories erected. Why does God have to have a chosen people? But that was dismissed. "Baby, that's just the devil whispering in your ear." Like a lullaby, her words eased my mind and erased all my doubts, allowing me to regain my balance so that I could cross back into familiar territory.

I was a devout witness of Jehovah, about as devout as a five-year-old could be. But my faith would be tested by the time I was seven. By then I was living with my father, who was Muslim; and like all fathers, he wanted his son to follow in his footsteps. It was then that I was introduced to Islam. This was no easy task for my father. Like a gentle breeze, my grandmother's voice caressed my mind: "Terrell, those questions are doubt, and doubt is just the devil whispering in your ear." Her words were border guards constantly on the watch for the trespass of doubt. They gave me courage and I would defend my fledgling beliefs. "Jesus Is God." I would say in defiance.

"No, son, Jesus was just a man." My father's words slowly slipped past that barrier that those Old Testament stories had constructed. After all, this was my father. How could the devil whisper through him? If it was the devil whispering through him, those whispers turned into shouts, drowning out my grandmother's voice.

My father's incursions past the border of my belief came in waves. He was relentless in his teaching of Islam. The first thing he did was give me a new Arabic name. As long as I was in his home I was Rafique, a name I hated. Rafique was foreign, and it sounded weird. He would call out to me, "Rafique!" He would use this fake Arabic accent and in the beginning, I would duck my head in shame.

Religion with my father was nothing like sitting at my grandmother's knee listening to stories from the Bible. It was work. There was no television, my father didn't own one at the time. But there were books, and to my young eyes it seemed like hundreds of them lined the tall bookshelf in my father's home. So, at the age of seven, my days consisted of reading. It was not the typical Dr. Seuss, *Cat in the Hat* books, they were books on Islam. For hours, I had to sit upstairs in my room reading and memorizing passages from those books. I then had to come downstairs and recite what I had memorized. *Islam is a way of life, as old as man himself.* It's funny how forty years later I can still recall the first sentence of the first book I had to memorize. Anyway, if I forgot a sentence, I was sent back upstairs until I got it right. I also had to learn how to pray in another language and remember the English translation. Islam was difficult for me. What seven-year-old would enjoy reading all those boring books and waking up at the crack of dawn to pray? I know I didn't. Although I struggled with what my father taught me, I had to learn. So, I learned Arabic, I learned how to pray, I memorized those passages, I learned to accept the discipline that was required to pray five times a day, and eventually I got used to being called Rafique. Before I knew it, my father's teachings successfully infiltrated my borders of belief and a new boundary was established, along with the construction of an unbreakable wall. I was trapped behind this border, harboring secret desires of crossing back into a world of old rugs, the odor of Ben Gay, and my grandmother's voice spinning tales of the Old Testament.

My father was proud of me because I became the perfect little Muslim. But if he had known what I prayed for every day, five times a day, he never would have introduced me to Islam. I didn't pray for toys or the ability to run fast or jump high. My prayers were a plea to Allah for that wall to come down so that I could go back across that border to leave behind my father's home, the hard work and discipline of Islam, and the name Rafique. It was a prayer to be back in Jehovah's world, back to my mother, back to being Terrell, where I could once more lose myself in those stories of the Old Testament, sitting at my grandmother's knee.

Twelve months to the day that I arrived at my father's home, my prayers were answered and I was back with my mother's family. But instead of the border being removed and the wall being destroyed, a new border was created, along with an even higher wall topped with razor wire. With my father, no longer around to make sure I maintained my discipline, almost immediately, my interest moved to other things. But those things didn't include being a witness or listening to those Old Testament stories. Those things were for babies. As an eight-year-old, my time had been hijacked by the rough-and-tumble life of a third grader. There was a neighborhood to explore, bugs to catch, girls to chase, slingshots to make, and games to play. Every day another brick and more razor wire were added to the wall, and I became further and further removed from that five-year-old witness and that seven-year-old Muslim. Beyond this new barrier, religion had become a whisper among the loud voices of life. And by the time I was a young adult, only an echo remained. You see, how to survive the streets became the most important to me. There was no need in my life for those Old Testament stories. Moses splitting the Red Sea, Jonah being swallowed by a whale, Lot's wife turning into a pillar of salt or Sampson destroying that Philistine's home were stories that had no practical applications for me. My life and the struggle to take care of myself was paramount. Those stories were simply that—stories told a child sitting at his grandmother's knee. What my father taught me fared no better. Nothing that I memorized in those books taught me how to smoke weed, drink alcohol or become falling-down high from codeine consumption. No matter how often I prayed, I couldn't shake the influence of those streets. The borders that I had enclosed myself in were heavily patrolled and religion was not allowed.

Throughout my life there have been all kinds of borders that I've had to navigate. Some of them were self-imposed, others imposed upon me. Some I've been able to cross, while others have been uncrossable, and religion has been all these things.

My grandmother and father have both passed on, crossing that ultimate border of no return. It's been more than ten years now, and a lot of my memories of them are beginning to fade. But what has remained strong in my mind is my grandmother's voice spinning those Old Testament tales, the feeling of that old worn-down rug and the smell of muscle rub. I can clearly recall the sound of my father's voice booming throughout the house, "Rafique!" and the pride in his eyes when he listened to me recite a prayer in Arabic. Although at the time I hated studying those Islamic books, what I know now is that in forcing me to memorize those passages, my father had given me the greatest gift of all—the love of the written word. So, every time I pick up a book, every time I write something new, my father is there with me nodding his head in approval. As impossible a barrier death may be, somehow both my grandmother and my father are able to circumvent its borders. Although they're gone, what they taught me about religion and how they taught it to me are the parts of them that continuously cross that border of no return, keeping them alive in my heart and mind.

INCARCERATION

OF TEARS

The eyes of the courtroom wept streams of sunlight that filtered through the curtain cracks, highlighting a swarm of dust particles that floated lazily in the air. The movement of the dust had a slow-motion effect, and it could become hypnotizing if you stared too long. Slowly, I dragged my eyes away. I paused as I got this weird sensation that the sunlight was freedom, and to look away would be to lose it.

I continued to look away, my eyes finally coming to rest on the judge sitting high up on his throne-like bench. Wrinkles creased his forehead. He was studying some papers on his desk. All I could see were those wrinkles and the top of his balding, age-spotted head. My mind began to wander: what if I'm found guilty? I could feel the pounding of my heart as its rate increased. My mouth became bone-dry while sweat covered my palms and trickled slowly down my back. Anxiety had invited fear to take up residence within my soul, and anger was pounding on the front door. I took a quick glance behind me at the rows of seats filled with family and friends. Could my loved ones see my fear? Did my face betray my anxiety? I struggled to keep my face blank; after all, I had an image to uphold – powerful, soldier, thug, afraid of nothing, one who looks fear in the eye and spits in its face.

Always "the man," I donned my mask of indifference. I smirked, something I always do when I want to hide my fear. Right at that moment, I locked eyes with my five-year-old baby sister. She called out my name and reached her tiny arms out for me. What could I do? I couldn't go to her. I couldn't pick her up. I couldn't place kisses on her cheeks. I could feel the desperation of my tears as they struggled to be free from the prison that my eyes had become. I took a deep breath and secured the locks of their incarceration, blew my baby sister a kiss, and faced forward again with my image still intact.

Not a second had passed before the judge peered over his horn-rimmed glasses. He stared at me as if he could see through me. He cleared his throat. A hush fell over the courtroom. There was no emotion in those cold, blue eyes or his voice. "Mr. Carter, would you please stand?" Now, not only could I feel my heart pounding, I could hear it vibrating against my eardrums. The judge continued, "I find you guilty of murder in the second degree, which carries a mandatory sentence of life without parole."

The courtroom erupted into shouts and cries of despair. My father, uncles, aunts, brothers, sisters, and friends all stood. Fingers of accusation were pointed like arrows at the judge. The sudden shift in mood made the sheriffs nervous. Like the shiftiness of a hummingbird in flight, their eyes darted back and forth; searching the crowd for signs of trouble as they quickly surrounded me.

When the judge uttered those words that robbed me of my freedom, time stopped; I became trapped in that moment—not by the judge's words, but by the pandemonium in that courtroom. Now twenty years later, the commotion of that day has settled in my mind, and the judge's words of condemnation are one of two things that I remember so vividly. But at the time, those words had little impact on me. It was because of the scream. Like the terrifying wail of an air-raid siren warning people that bombs were dropping from the sky, a cry erupted from my mother. This scream silenced all other voices in that courtroom. It was unadulterated pain fathered by tragedy that manifested in a sound I can only describe as a guttural scream soaked in wretchedness and dragged through an alley of anguish. Everything ceased to exist except my mother and me. This scream seemed to emanate from a place deep within her that only a woman who had given birth would know. Never in my life have I experienced the hurt that I felt at hearing this sound that came from the woman who kissed me on the cheek, tucked me in the bed, and chased the bogeyman away. It sliced through me, cutting me deep to my core.

The atmosphere in that courtroom was filled with sorrow, and self-pity thickened it. It was hard for me to breathe. My throat became tight and I swallowed. But at that point, it was all about me. The grief in that courtroom became a coat that I cloaked myself in, shielding myself from the chill of responsibility. Why me? The DA is a racist. The judge is a racist. This wouldn't happen to me if I was white. I was so engrossed in my self-pity that I failed to take into account my actions and what part I played in the circumstances that I found myself in.

Suddenly, it was as if God wanted to show me how self-pity blinded me to responsibility – and that my mother's pain was an old agony and her wail was a cry that had been echoing across this land for centuries. Gradually, the commotion in the courtroom began to fade. There was a white blinding light and I could feel a sensation of disembodiment. I was floating, connected to nothing. A myriad of colors was shooting pass me, then, the reality that I knew was gone.

I had been dropped off into a place that time seemed to forget: Gray clouds fill the skies and the rain falls in a misty haze. I stand as a child shivering in my mother's arms upon a wooden auction block. The judge now is a slave auctioneer. His cold blue eyes latch on to me, sizing me up like a calf on its way to the butcher. He sneers. There is no humanity in that sneer or those arctic seas of blue, no compassion, no mercy. Pale hands reach out. They are huge, growing larger as my fear amplifies them. I flinch right before he grabs me. His hands are cold, hard, and the calluses that cover his palms scrape against the naked flesh of my bare shoulder.

I shiver from the cold of his touch and my fear. He squeezes tight and his vise-like grip sends pain shooting down the length of my arm. I cry out, but my cries are the cries of the calf being sold to the butcher. They are just noises of an animal. What does the butcher care for the cries of his food? Then I'm snatched away from the safety of my mother's arms. "We got one healthy nigger boy-child. Let the bidding began at two bits." Dozens of white faces stand in front of the auction block leering at me, and when the thick southern drawl of the auctioneer's voice commences the bidding, hands shoot in the air and competing shouts of purchase erupt from the crowd. In a matter of seconds, life as I know it will be over. I will be sold to another human being who hates me, moved to a place unknown, never to see my mother again.

My mother, tears streaming down her face, reaches out for me, but her motherly instinct to protect me is answered by a savage kick to the face and an unmerciful beating. This brave African woman still cries out, not from the pain of the beating, but from the agony of losing her firstborn son.

I guess God deemed my lesson learned, and it was; for I was able to see through the eyes of the truly condemned that bled their innocence on the wooden planks of an auction block. I could feel the pain of my ancestors who lost their freedom through no fault of their own, who, through the following centuries, paved a path with their lives so that I could be free. Free to do what, though? Take for granted the lives sacrificed for my own, so that I could then relinquish the freedom that others died for? Who am I to feel sorry for myself? I'm the one who brought to life our tortured past to be relived through the misery of a mother losing her firstborn son. It was I who opened the door of my mother's soul, allowing the echoed agony of our ancestors to vibrate through her heart.

The tragedy of that auction block began to fade. God picked me up again and carried me out of that time where my predecessors lived and died as chattel.

We traveled along the echoes of my mother's cry, passing through a deluge of shame that soaked me to my core. A barrage of colors passed before my eyes. There was a faint sound of voices. They became louder and, just as I realized what I was hearing, I was dumped back into the commotion of that courtroom.

At that point, my mother's scream began a symphony of grief. It was a sad melody that infiltrated my entire being, building up to a cacophony of dissonant chords of emotions within my soul. Tired of knocking, anger burst through the door of my anxiety, and fear. I just wanted to shout, *"I ain't dead, y'all, stop fucking crying!"*

At twenty-three, I just couldn't understand the enormity of the circumstance. I couldn't understand what was obvious to everyone else in that courtroom: that there now existed a very strong possibility that I would never see the outside of a prison wall again. Was I in denial? I don't think so. It was just that life-without-parole was so far outside of my life experience that I had no way of knowing what it meant. To me, five years was a lifetime, so the idea of spending the remainder of my life behind a prison wall was just too alien for me to understand. I was lost, my youth blinding me to the concept of time.

Instead of shouting, though, I simply dropped my head and told the sheriff, "Yo, get me the fuck out of here." The handcuffs clicking around my wrist, in a perverse way, felt comfortable because it signaled my exit out of that maelstrom of grief. A slight nudge by the sheriff and I began the long walk down that center aisle of sorrow.

I avoided looking at the faces of my loved ones. The anguish and the tears were just too much to bear. I could feel my incarcerated tears once again begin their struggle to break free from the prison of my eyes, and once again I secured their locks. I couldn't let my family see that kind of weakness in me. After all, grown men don't cry, do they? I took a quick glance to my right. Oh, shit! Are those tears streaming down my father's face? Naw, that has to be my eyes playing tricks on me. I quickly faced forward again, resisting the urge to look his way again. At the time, I couldn't deal with a challenge to my concept of manhood.

This idea of what a man is and how he conducts himself during times of stress is what I clung to in order to maintain my composure and sanity. My machismo was my strength; the warrior in me enabled me to fight. Tears streaming down my father's face would have destroyed this idea. The very foundation that would have given me the strength and the will to fight would be no more and I would have fallen into a black hole of despair. So instead, I kept my eyes glued to the top of the exit where portraits of old white men hung, those whose judgments populated penitentiary graveyards across the state. Who are these men? And why can't I see myself in those images. Instead, I'm reminded of the men handcuffed and shamed who've walked this path before and how they all look like me. Before I could fully explore this thought, I entered the City Hall corridor.

As soon as I stepped into that hallway, time slowed and a moment became an eternity. Another one of my sisters, just a few years younger than I, was doubled over in agony, sobs wracking her body and tears pouring from her eyes. Then she looked up. The hurt that was etched across her face became seared into my mind, a constant reminder of the terrible pain I caused. It was at that moment, as I locked eyes with my sister, unable to comfort her, that I realized that my life and how I lived it not only affected me but affected other people as well. My anxiety and fear were so distracted by anger bursting through the front door, that they were totally unaware when sorrow crept through the back to take sole possession of my soul. The sheriff nudged me forward again, and the tears that I had been holding prisoner finally broke free. I couldn't incarcerate them anymore. Liberated, they covered my face with signs of their escape.

FOR ANY COMMENTS OR QUESTIONS
PLEASE CONTACT THE AUTHOR
:
TERRELL CARTER BZ-5409
P.O. BOX 244
GRATERFORD, PA 19426

www.ingramcontent.com/pod-product-compliance
Lightning Source LLC
Chambersburg PA
CBHW072000170626
46813CB00005B/1941